D0615997

BLACK DIAMOND

BLACK DIAMOND

BRITTANI WILLIAMS

www.urbanbooks.net

Urban Books, LLC
1199 Straight Path
West Babylon, NY 11704

ISBN-13: 978-1-60162-265-5
ISBN-10: 1-60162-265-1

First Mass Market Printing March 2010
First Trade Paperback Printing December 2009
Printed in the United States of America

10   9   8   7   6   5   4   3

This is a work of fiction. Any references or similarities to actual events, real people, living, or dead, or to real locales are intended to give the novel a sense of reality. Any similarity in other names, characters, places, and incidents is entirely coincidental.

Distributed by Kensington Publishing Corp.
Submit Wholesale Orders to:
Kensington Publishing Corp.
C/O Penguin Group (USA) Inc.
Attention: Order Processing
405 Murray Hill Parkway
East Rutherford, NJ 07073-2316
Phone: 1-800-526-0275
Fax: 1-800-227-9604

BLACK DIAMOND

Chapter One

Diamond: Who's Betraying Who?

I heard the moaning loudly through the halls and had I not been standing here myself I would have never believed it. Two people that I trusted, the two people that I would have taken a bullet for, were right there in my home betraying me. Sorry would never be enough to ease my pain, and at that point there was no turning back. My footsteps couldn't be heard over their loud lovemaking, and not even the door opening interrupted them. I stood there in the dark hallway watching. Hell, I figured I might as well let them finish before I let my presence be known. At least then it would all be worth it. As Kemp laid flat on his back, his arms tightly gripped Mica's waist. She grinded into him and let out moans each time the strokes hit her spot. The flickering of the candlelight bounced off of her body, making it radiant. Even the beads of sweat that formed on her back were evident.

Though I was furious, I can admit that watching the two of them in action was slightly turning me on. Under different circumstances I would have gladly joined in, but I had to focus on the action at hand. She continued to ride him jockey style and soon he was yelling her name and palming her ass until he had expelled every drop of his love inside of her.

She slowed her pace and after stopping I knew that it was my cue. I raised my gun and aimed in their direction. I released the safety, which quickly gained their attention. Mica jumped off of him and began backing up to the top of the bed, covering her naked body with the sheets. Kemp sat up in shock and spoke immediately, trying to calm me down.

"Baby, it's not what you think," he spat, the same bullshit line that every man speaks when they get caught. What the fuck did he think—I was blind? I clearly walked into this room and saw him fucking my best friend and all his stupid ass could say was that it's not what I think.

"What kind of asshole do you think that I am?" I screamed, trying not to lose my cool. "Did you actually think you could get away with this?"

"I'm so sorry you had to see this. I never wanted you to find out this way!" Mica cried, as tears began pouring out of her eyes. "I didn't want to hurt you."

"You didn't want to hurt me? That's bullshit! Fucking my man is definitely not the way to avoid it. I trusted you and this is what I get?" I pointed the gun again.

"Please, Diamond. Don't do this. This is not the way to handle this," Kemp continued to try his hand.

"Fuck you! You don't have the right to tell me what to do and what not to do. I'm running this shit! Do you see this gun—remember this sight cause this is the last thing that you are going to see. I hope the pussy was worth it!" I cocked the gun and began shooting, releasing five shots. The blood spraying all of the room was something that I would never forget, somewhat like a bad dream that seemed too real not to believe. I would take this to the grave.

I never wanted to resort to murder. Hell, I wasn't a criminal. Well, not a convicted one anyway. I worked hard to get to the point where I was today and I didn't plan on letting anyone take me down. You never really know the things that lie ahead for you but all of the choices you make ultimately have an effect on the way things turn out. Looking back on the way I grew up, most would say that they wouldn't have expected anything different from me. I, on the other hand, expected much more.

I was adopted at the age of two and it wasn't until I was ten that my mother decided to reveal the truth. I knew I didn't fit the mold of the family from the beginning but I never had any concrete proof. After my mother and father divorced we moved in with my grandmother to a small row house in North Philly. In total, there were about five houses on the block occupied by humans. The rest were boarded up and infested with rodents, most of which the crackheads used as shelter to get high. My mother always said that eventually we would move on to bigger and better things, but *eventually* never happened.

My grandmom had lived there all of her life and refused to move. Shit, she still had the old sofas with the plastic on them, so you know she wasn't going anywhere. We weren't the only ones in the family that had run to Grandmom's for shelter. There was my aunt Cicely who swore her shit didn't stink. She was on welfare and worked under the table at the hair salon as a shampoo girl. She was the reason the working class hated paying taxes, since she was more than capable of getting a full-time job but she'd rather collect money from the government to go clubbing every weekend. She barely saw her children since they were stuck in the house with my grandmom most of the time. Her idea of quality time was stopping in and giving them a few new toys. It was bullshit to me; I figured that anyone who wasn't capable of being a good parent should never have kids.

It was rough in the neighborhood. Resisting temptation was the hardest. With all of the drugs and things around, how could I not get involved? I know that sounds like bull, but try living in the world of sin and see if you'll come out of it a saint. I didn't have a lot of friends in the neighborhood because girls weren't my choice of companionship. I was into boys early, which only got me into trouble.

I met Mica through her brother, Johnny. Johnny and I met after we both were caught stealing from the supermarket. There was a room in the back of the store where they would hold you until your parents arrived. I sat there quietly waiting for my mom to come and watched as Johnny cried buckets of tears. He must have been scared of an ass whooping or something because he was definitely a little extra with his reaction.

"Are you okay?" I asked, trying to get him to stop crying, because he was annoying the hell out of me.

"Yeah, I'm fine!" he replied, turning his face in the opposite direction.

"What's got you so upset? I mean, damn, is the beating going to be that bad?" I asked, still not done probing him for information.

"Why do you care? You don't even know me," he replied.

"I know that, but I'm tired of hearing you cry like a little girl, so I'm trying to make small talk to get you to shut up!"

"What?" he replied, turning to look at me.

"You heard me! Stop crying like a little girl!" I yelled.

He jumped up out of his chair and ran over to where I was sitting. Soon, we were rolling around on the floor fighting like two cartoon characters. It was probably comical seeing us trying to hold the other one's hands down. He wasn't really that much stronger than me, but I didn't really feel like fighting. I simply wanted him to shut up.

"Get your hands off of me," I yelled, struggling to get my hands loose. "I knew you were a little girl, boys don't fight girls!"

"They do when girls don't know how to keep quiet," he yelled, not releasing his grip on my wrists.

"You know you like it, you like a girl that's slick with the tongue," I said, trying to make him lose his concentration.

"What?" He loosened his grip for a second, and that was all I needed to get the upper hand. I flipped him over and was now sitting on top of him holding his hands down.

"Now, why don't you just give up? I got you now," I said, looking him in the eyes as he tried to get loose.

Just then the door opened and his father and sister came in with the security guard from the store.

"What is going on here? Get off of him!" his father yelled.

I quickly got up and moved over to the chair that I had been sitting in before our fight started.

"Nothing, Dad. We were just playing," he lied.

"Just playing my ass, you know how much trouble you're in right now?"

"Yes, Dad," he answered after getting up from the floor.

"Let's go. Don't worry, he'll never steal anything from your store again," his dad said to the security guard as they headed out of the room.

I felt sorry for him because I could tell that he was afraid of his father. It was a few weeks before I ran into his sister. I was walking to the corner store to buy a loaf of bread for my grandmom when I saw Mica. She looked at me strangely before coming over to talk to me. I thought for sure that she was going to want to fight since she walked in on me and her brother, but I was surprised by what she had to say.

"You're the girl that was in that security room with my brother, right?"

"Yeah, that's me. Why?" I asked, preparing for a throw-down.

"Girl, what's your name? My brother hasn't stopped talking about you since that day. I think he's in love," she said, laughing.

I stood there for a second in shock. In love? *After the way I talked to him, he must be crazy,* I thought. Then I replied, "My name is Diamond. What did he say about me?"

"He just said that he liked your style and you were sly with your mouth but he could deal with that."

"That's crazy, he really said that?" I asked. Now I was blushing because though I thought he was a little punk, he was cute. He wouldn't be able to protect me but he was good to look at, as long as he wasn't crying.

"Yeah, he did. My name is Mica and his name is Johnny. We live right over there on Dover Street. Why don't you come hang out with us sometime? We're always outside."

"I might just do that. Thanks, Mica, I'll be seeing you around soon," I said before turning to head into the store.

Soon Mica and I were best friends and Johnny was my first love. I found out that their father was really abusive and Johnny got it the worst. He was afraid of his father and that was why he cried that day in the supermarket. Johnny was really calm, not like all of the other boys I had dealt with. Most of them already had a sample of sex so they didn't really care about quality time and conversation.

Johnny, on the other hand, did. We would talk on the phone for hours every night about anything you could think of.

During this time Mica and I hung out a lot too. We got really close but grew closer before Johnny got locked up for murder. After years of abuse he was finally fed up and in a rage he shot and killed their father. I was shocked when Mica called and told me the news. I was even more shocked that she blamed part of it on me. She said that it was me that pushed him to do it. I knew I had nothing to do with it. Johnny was fed up; all I did was encourage him. I never wanted him to be afraid of anyone. I hated that he was being abused. Shit, if anything she should have thanked me. It saved her from being beaten too.

A few months later Mica and her mother moved out of the neighborhood to somewhere in Delaware County. It would be years before I would see Mica again, and now that I think of it, it may have been better if I'd never seen her at all. Then I wouldn't be in my home covered with her blood. Damn, what happened to the good old days?

Chapter Two

Mica: Dreams

I hated the long ride up to the Camp Hill Prison, but I had to show my brother love. Besides the fact that we didn't have much family, most of the family we had didn't want to see him. I knew my brother too well and had it not been for him falling too deep in love he would have never been in prison in the first place. Though it had been five years since the day he murdered my father it still felt like yesterday.

I was only fifteen the day they hauled him off to prison. At the time I didn't get a true sense of what was happening, but it didn't take long for me to figure it out. As time passed I realized that both my father and brother were gone. Johnny wasn't dead but he was gone from the life that I'd been used to. That gunshot, to me, killed two birds with one stone. Most of my family completely erased him from their life. I loved him too much to treat him the way that they had. Where others couldn't forgive him, I did. The person I couldn't forgive was the bitch who pushed him to do it. I mean, I've been in love—don't get me wrong—but if there is a love that can make you kill your own parent, then I don't want it.

After I arrived and checked in to see my brother I had to sit and wait until they brought him down to the visiting area. I was anxious to get this visit over with because I had a date with a fine-ass hustler that I couldn't miss. I know that sounds inconsiderate, but shit, a girl's gotta do what a girl's gotta do. He might be the key that would finally get me out of the fucked-up neighborhood we called home.

As my brother entered the room, I smiled. I missed my Johnny so much and even the letters weren't enough to make me feel the closeness that we once had. He had gotten so big in prison and had turned into a man. It saddened me that he had to grow up this way.

"Hey, baby sis!" he said, smiling and looking me up and down as if he hadn't just seen me last week. I made it my business to get up there every week no matter what else I had to do. In my book, family came first. Everything else was secondary.

"What's up?" I said, reaching out to give him a quick hug. Hugging wasn't really allowed but the guards were cool and would allow it for a second. "Did you get the money I sent last week after I left?"

"Yeah, I got it. I told you not to do that. You are supposed to be saving that money for school," he replied, sitting down on the opposite side of the table.

"Johnny, when are you going to give up? I'm not going to school. I told you that I'm going to be all right without that. Shit, Mom can barely make ends meet so the little bit of money I make working at the mall I give to her. I can't see you in here without, so I do what I have to do. You know me, always looking out for the family."

"Yeah, I know, but sometimes you got to look out for yourself."

"I will soon, trust me; I have something in the works."

"Like what? I hope it's not illegal. I don't want to see you behind bars too. One of us is enough."

"No, it's not illegal. You know I'm not into shit like that," I responded, twisting my lip because I wasn't hardly trying to do anything that would land me in jail. I wasn't that damn crazy.

"Just checking but hey, have you seen or heard from Diamond yet? Or checked on her old address? I still haven't gotten a response from her. I must have sent her hundreds of letters since I been here."

"Hell no, I haven't seen her and that's the way I want to keep it. You know how I feel about her," I replied, annoyed that he would even say her name to me. Just the mention of her made my skin crawl.

"I wish you would stop blaming her for what I did. I made my own decision, Mica; she didn't have anything to do with what I did. I don't have any family that keeps in contact with me but you. I asked you to find out where she was so that I can have some contact with the outside world. That's all I've ever asked you to do for me."

"You can say what you want, but the bottom line is that you wouldn't be here if it wasn't for her and you know that I'm telling the truth."

"Neither of us knows if that's true. Who knows what I would have done if I was pushed hard enough?"

"Look, Johnny, I came a long way and I damn sure don't want to waste our visiting time talking about her."

"Well, I'll drop it for now but you're still going to have to find a way to let the past go and move on. You can't be bitter all your life. Shit, I'm the one in jail."

I wasn't bitter but I didn't want to keep the debate going. I could care less about Diamond and if I saw her on the street it would probably be as if I never knew her. I know you are supposed to forgive, but I couldn't find it in me. How could I forgive the person that ruined my family? It was definitely easier said than done and yes, he was the one in jail, but for years I felt like I was there with him. Things weren't all peachy on the outside either. My mother struggled with depression and had been on medication for it since my father died. Some people thought that Johnny did all of us a favor, but neither she nor I saw it that way. Yes, he was abusive and yes he was an undercover drug addict, but he kept us afloat. Now, if it weren't for my little part-time job we probably wouldn't even have food to eat. I hated that he was gone. I didn't miss getting my ass whooped but I missed being a kid. I had to grow up quickly in order to make it. I had to learn how to take care of myself when my mother was too depressed to get out of bed. She hadn't been there to talk about sex or anything for that matter. She was like a shell with no life, and nothing I did was bringing her back.

I finished chatting with my brother for the remainder of his visiting time and headed back out to the bus that drove back to Philly. Since moving from North Philly we lived in a two-bedroom apartment in Germantown. I mean, if there was a hood in Philly worse than North Philly it was Germantown. The craziest part about the chicks up there was that you couldn't tell them they weren't hot shit even when their doors on their houses were practically hanging off the hinge. I got into more fights the two years I went to Germantown High than I had in my whole life. I had never been afraid to speak my mind so whenever they had something to say I came back with the truth. Obviously, the truth hurt and they would wait for me after school each time. I always came out prepared for a fight since most days I got into some sort of altercation during school hours.

I hated the school just as much as I hated my life, and there had been plenty of times when I thought about swallowing a bottle of pills to end it all. But then I thought about my mother and how devastating that would have been to her, especially since my brother was locked up. I realized that keeping her as sane as I could was more important and that thinking of taking my own life was just me being selfish.

On the ride home all I could think about was the date that I was about to go on. I felt that I was finally going to get a slice of the pie. Living the fabulous life was something that I dreamed of. The difference with me was that I wanted the man with money but the money wasn't the most important. I wanted a man to be happy, which was something that I hadn't had in a long time.

Soon, we were pulling up in the bus station and I was smiling from ear to ear. I couldn't wait to get home to get dressed and head out for my date. It took me another hour on buses to get home and once I made it I hurried to my room to rummage through my clothes. I hadn't bought anything new in a while, so I had to mix and match to try and make the perfect outfit. Finally, I settled on a black pencil skirt that was fitted and reached my knee with a black-and-white shirt that showed just the right amount of cleavage. You know, enough to make his mouth water but not too much that he'd think I was a slut. My mother must have heard all of the commotion going on in my room. You would have thought I had company the way I was dancing around and giggling like a kid.

"What the hell is all the noise in here about?" she asked, opening my door and looking in to see that I was alone.

"I'm just happy, Mom. That's all."

"Happy? What the hell are you so happy about?"

"I have a date tonight and this guy might make a difference in both of our lives."

"Don't you go letting some nigga sell you a dream. Most times they are lying anyway."

"Mom, stop being so negative all the time. Can't you at least be happy for me?"

Without saying a word she turned and walked away. I knew that she didn't want me to get hurt. Hell, that definitely wasn't my intention, but shit happens and if it wasn't meant to be I'm sure that I would find out soon enough. Tonight, I wasn't going to focus on her negative energy but on seeing the man that I knew in my heart was going to make all of my dreams come true. I know that sounds corny but it was true. Tyson was supposed to pick me up at nine and I made sure that I was ready. I had borrowed some of my mom's Miracle perfume and put on just enough accessories to accentuate the outfit that I had put together. On my way out my mom told me to be careful, but she still didn't crack a smile. Damn, I hated depression!

Nine-oh-five, Tyson was beeping the horn and I couldn't have gotten out to his car fast enough. I'd had so many disappointments so I prayed that today wouldn't be one of those times. Tyson sat in the driver's seat, speaking on the phone and unlocked the doors once I got close. I thought he could have at least opened the door for me, but maybe being a gentleman wasn't in his character. That didn't mean he was a bad guy, though, because all of the other nuts I dated opened the door but once they got some, all of that shit was gone. At least he wasn't trying to impress me by being extra, and that was definitely a plus in my book. Who the hell opens the door for you nowadays anyway?

He turned briefly and looked at my ass as I sat down—a typical guy, but I loved it. He continued his conversation as I buckled my seat belt and he drove off. I didn't even know where the hell he was taking me, but at that point it didn't even matter. I was just happy to be around him.

"I don't give a fuck what he said, I know he better have that man money right!" he yelled, frowning. "Well, where is he?" He continued his ranting as I sat quietly, trying not to look in his direction though I was trying to hear what the person was saying on the opposite end. "Well hit me up, I got some shit to take care of right now. Make sure you get all the money! One!" He hung up and immediately turned his attention to me. "What's up, sexy? Sorry about that; niggas always call me at the worst time with dumb shit."

"I know the feeling," I lied. I didn't know anything about what he was talking about, but I thought it would sound cute if I said I did.

"I see you got all dressed up, I'm feeling the outfit," he said, smiling, showing his softer side. You wouldn't have known he had one by the conversation he just had on the phone, but I guess business was business.

"Yeah, I tried to look sexy for you tonight."

"Well, you did a damn good job, sweetie."

"So where are we going?"

"Over to my spot. I had a caterer hook up a crazy spread. I got some Moët and all that shit over there too."

I smiled but inside I was a little uneasy. Over to his spot? I could see where this was going to lead. I wasn't trying to have sex with him tonight; I wanted to get to know him. Most times when you have sex with someone so fast you never learn anything about them because the relationship stays sexual. Well, I guess I had to hope for the best because I wasn't going to turn back now.

"Cool," I said, after a few seconds of thinking.

He bobbed his head to the sounds of his Jay-Z CD. I loved his swagger. I felt like he could protect me, and that was also something that I yearned for. He had on a baseball cap tilted to the side with jeans and a black button-up shirt. His diamond Cartier watch continued to sparkle even in the night. His chain had diamonds bigger than any I had ever seen and his earring was just as big as those in his chain. The jewelry that he donned probably cost more than my entire wardrobe. His mustache and beard were jet-black and shaped up perfectly, not a hair out of place. His skin was golden brown like a glazed doughnut and his cologne filled the air with an irresistible scent. He kept peeking over at me from time to time during the drive. He even reached over and grabbed my hand when he wasn't on the phone cussing someone out about money. Witnessing that showed me that money didn't erase all of your problems. It only brought new ones.

Tyson was a drug dealer who did pretty well. I didn't know who he worked for, but whoever he was Tyson made sure he stayed loyal and everyone that worked under him did as well. I didn't know firsthand how hard that must be, feeling the weight of all of your men. Since, if one of them messed up Tyson would be the one to pay for their mistakes.

I met Tyson while hanging out in the area where he did most of his business. One of his workers was actually going to rob me, but Tyson stopped them and told me how dangerous it was to hang in that part of town. I didn't really take heed to that. Shit, I figured that since Tyson stopped them once they wouldn't try me again. I was wrong, and it took me almost getting raped before I did. Tyson stepped in again and drove me home. We talked that night and he took my number before I got out of the car. It took him a few days to call but once he did we set up the date that we were on now. I guess I was in the right place at the right time because I probably would have never met him otherwise.

Once we pulled up in front of his house my stomach started doing flips. I was nervous about going in because I wanted to keep him around. I didn't want to go in and have sex with him and he'd forget me by tomorrow. I mean, I had been told I was good in bed, but a man like him probably had women coming from left and right. There were probably some much more experienced than me who could get his attention at any given moment.

We got out and entered his house, which was so clean it looked like no one even lived there. I knew he must have had a maid or never stayed there because it was too perfect. Out of nowhere a huge black pit bull ran into the living room and jumped into his arms. I stood still, stiff as a board. I was so afraid of dogs, especially pit bulls, and it didn't matter how many times someone told me their dog didn't bite. Hell, they had teeth, which to me meant that they could bite whenever they wanted to.

"What, you scared? He ain't gonna hurt you," he laughed, noticing how petrified I was of the huge dog that weighed probably just as much as me.

"Yes, I'm afraid of dogs."

"Cool, I'll put him out back."

"Thanks," I said, still not budging and watching his every move.

I relaxed once I heard the back door open and close. He reappeared, still laughing. He walked into the dining room and gestured for me to follow behind him. I took a seat at the table that had plates laid out as if it were a restaurant. There was a bucket for champagne sitting in the center. He grabbed it off the table and returned it with ice and a bottle of Moët inside. He took the plates off of the table and brought them back a few minutes later filled with soul food—chicken, macaroni and cheese, and collard greens. I laughed at how I thought it would be something different. He had everything set up so classy I would have thought he would have a spread of food that I didn't even eat. I was cool with the food, though, and his money wouldn't go to waste.

We ate the food and drank so much Moët that I could barely stand. I was laughing at everything he said even when it wasn't funny. I was so relaxed. I had kicked off my shoes and got comfortable on the sofa as he put in a movie, *South Central,* a classic hood movie that I hadn't seen in a while. We sat and watched the movie as he massaged my feet. Soon, we were both asleep on the sofa. It was about one-thirty AM when he woke me up to take me up to the bedroom. I stumbled most of the way but made it and plopped down on his bed like a load of bricks. He helped me get undressed and put one of his T-shirts on me. I thought for sure he would make a move. Surprisingly, he didn't; he crawled into bed with me and fell asleep.

Chapter Three

Diamond: King of the World

As women, why do we settle for less? I had asked myself this question a million times and could never seem to come up with an acceptable answer. I had been through a lot in the five years after losing Johnny, my first love. After the day he went to jail I had never been able to find a man to treat me the way that he did. I know that we were just teenagers at the time, but shit, love is love no matter how you slice it.

Now, there I was, twenty-one, drop-dead gorgeous with a college degree, but still I settled for a man who didn't even care enough about me to protect himself when he went out and cheated. As I sat in the waiting area of the CVS Pharmacy, waiting on my prescription, I was about to explode. I was so angry that I could barely contain myself. I had just left my GYN for my recent test results and found out that I had chlamydia. I knew that I was faithful to Davey, my boyfriend of four years, so there was no other way that I could have contracted the disease. I had never been so embarrassed and once I left I planned on going straight to his house to give him a piece of my mind.

After I left the pharmacy I was on my way to his apartment. I called his cell phone a few times and when I didn't get an answer my instincts told me that he was up to no good. I couldn't hear anything else but the words that the doctor spoke before I left the office. It was like a broken record playing over and over again. Once I got to the door of Davey's apartment I began knocking. I waited a few minutes before knocking again. I knew he was home because his car was parked outside. I continued to knock and yell his name.

"I know you're in there. Open this fucking door!" I continued to scream, waiting for him to acknowledge the fact that I was standing outside acting like a damn fool. Soon, I heard him unlocking the door and I already had my fists balled up, ready to swing.

"What the hell is wrong with you, Diamond?" he asked, still trying to fix his clothing.

I pushed him out of the way and entered the apartment. I didn't make it very far before he grabbed ahold of me. "Get the fuck off of me, you dirty bastard!" I screamed, trying to get my arm free from his grip.

"What is going on?" he asked, still holding on tightly.

"I have chlamydia, you dirty motherfucker! That's what's going on!" I continued to yell. He still wouldn't let me go. I was sure that he had someone in there, and I was trying to get back to the bedroom to see exactly who it was.

"What? How did you get that?" he asked with a dumb expression on his face. He knew damn well how I had gotten it. I had never cheated on him and he knew that.

"Don't play dumb, Davey. You know damn well how I got it. I haven't fucked anyone else but you. I'm positive that you can't say the same!" He finally let go of my arm but blocked the hall that led to his bedroom. "Move out of the way. I want to see what nasty ho you have back there. I know you were in here fucking around!" I screamed, trying to push him out of the way. He was much stronger than me, so I knew that he would never let me get past. I wasn't about to give up trying, though.

"It ain't nobody back there, Diamond. Stop tripping. What did the doctor say?"

"Oh, now you're concerned? Fuck you! You don't give a damn about me, you can't even wrap your dick up when you go screw around." I began to break down. My anger was now turning into pain. As many times as I had caught him cheating on me I still hung around. If someone were to ask me why I loved him, I wouldn't be able to answer them. Honestly, I wasn't even sure if I really loved him; it could be that I was just used to the things he provided. I didn't know of any other way to live but broke in a broke-down neighborhood, and I wasn't ready to go back there.

I wanted the old Davey back. The Davey I met four years ago. I could remember that day as if it had just happened, and just the thought of it warmed my heart.

* * *

I had just left school and was headed to the bus stop with a group of friends. I wasn't feeling too good and was anxious to get home and lay down. I stood there on the corner not really paying attention to my surroundings but more so to the pain in my stomach. A black BMW pulled up on the side where I was standing and parked. The windows had full tint so I couldn't see who was inside. Soon, the windows began to reveal the driver behind the wheel of the luxury car. His eyes were pointed in my direction, but I tried to act as if I didn't notice him. I didn't want him to think I was money hungry, though I was always down to be treated to something nice. He motioned with his fingers, telling me to come over. I pointed at myself just to make certain that he really wanted me. I mean, I was pretty and had a nice figure, but I wasn't dressed all that spectacular and my hair was plainly pulled back in a ponytail. I would have never expected a man of his stature to want me.

He nodded his head yes and I slowly headed over to his car to find out what the mystery man had to say. He smiled as I got closer. He had skin the color of a Hershey's kiss and jet-black hair that was perfectly trimmed. His smile was accentuated with two dimples that made you smile just looking at him. Everything about his face looked perfect as if it were a painted picture. Not even a hair in his mustache was out of place. I wondered what the hell he wanted with a plain Jane like me.

"I won't bite. Come closer," he spoke in a deep tone that sent chills through my body.

I gave a little girlish giggle before moving closer.

Was it that obvious that I was nervous? I smiled and waited for him to speak again.

"What's your name?" he asked, still holding his position inside the car.

"Diamond," I replied, trying to put on the sexiest voice that I could muster up.

"Diamond. I like that name. It fits. Where are you headed?"

"I'm going home; I don't feel too good," I replied.

"Well, why don't you let me drop you off and once you're feeling better we can hang out?"

"I don't even know your name."

"My name is Davey. I'm sorry, sweetie. That was rude of me."

I didn't want to agree, even though it was rather rude. I was hesitant about getting in his car but the sooner I got home the better. I agreed to get in, saying a silent prayer that I would make it home safely. The inside had the new-car scent, and you could tell by looking around that it was recently purchased. I was impressed; I had never been in a luxury car and it was definitely something I could get used to. My body was so comfortable in the plush leather seats that I almost forgot I was sick. Funny how a man can do that to you.

"So how old are you, Diamond?" he asked, trying to make small talk as we headed toward my neighborhood. I smiled as I noticed all of the neighborhood chicks trying to peer through the tinted windows to see who was inside.

"I'm seventeen. I graduate high school next month," I replied.

"That's what's up. I'm glad to hear that because

I would have had to back away if you were any younger." He laughed.

Within a few minutes we were pulling up to my house. I wanted to stay, but I knew I had to go. I didn't want to seem desperate, so I thanked him for the ride and told him I would be seeing him around. I was surprised he went through the trouble to bring me home and allowed me to dismiss him without even giving him my phone number.

A few hours later I was still lying down, trying to rest, hoping that my run of sickness would go away by the end of the night. The doorbell rang and I hurried down the stairs, unsure of who it was. My grandmom and I were the only ones home, and I wasn't expecting any visitors.

"Who is it?" I yelled, because in this neighborhood you could never be too sure.

"I have a delivery for a Ms. Diamond," the voice responded.

I slowly opened the door to a huge bouquet of pink roses with a pink and white teddy bear tied to the vase. I signed for the delivery and quickly shut the door to see who the hell sent this to me. I was sure that there had to be some mistake because no one would send me flowers. Or would they?

The card read:

To my Diamond in the rough,
Get better so I can show the world my new
girl.
Love, Davey

Okay, he has to be crazy, I thought. *His new girl?* I didn't even know him. The gesture was definitely appreciated since no one had ever done something so nice for me, but who the hell did he think he was? King of the world? I put the flowers and teddy bear in my room and soon after that I fell asleep.

He wouldn't give up, and it was that determination that turned me on. He managed to always keep me hanging on, hoping that the sweet guy I met that day would come back. I was fooled because the scene we were at right now had been repeated so many times. I guess love will do that to you.

I sat down on his sofa because I refused to leave the apartment until I knew who he was in here with. He came over and sat down beside me. I didn't even want him to touch me. I felt disgusting and the pain I felt at this point was probably worse than any other time before.

"What are you doing?" he asked, probably wondering why I had sat down.

"I'm not leaving until I see who's in here! I mean that shit, so you might as well bring the bitch out here," I responded as I eased back and crossed my legs. I know that I had been a fool in the past, but I'd be damned it he was going to get away with this one.

"Babe, I told you there is nobody back there. You need to stop being so fucking suspicious!"

"Suspicious? I just told you I have an STD. If that's not a reason to distrust you then I don't know what the hell is. You need to stop being so fucking trifling and wrap your dick up!" I retorted.

I still hadn't budged from the sofa, though I wanted to jump up and hit his ass.

"Oh, so now I'm trifling? Well, why are you with me then, Diamond? Am I trifling when you're out spending my money?"

"That doesn't have anything to do with this, Davey. Don't try and turn the heat on me. I haven't done anything wrong," I was well aware of his strategy to try and change the subject, but it wasn't going to work this time.

"I'm tired of arguing with you, Diamond. If you're gonna step, then step!" he yelled while motioning his hands at the door.

"What?" I yelled. I was furious. Here, he was the one who messed around and he was telling me to step. I looked around for something to throw. My eyes landed on a basketball trophy he had sitting on his end table. Without thinking twice, I picked it up off the table and threw it at him. He didn't have enough time to duck so it hit him on the side of his head. Next thing I knew I was back on the couch with his hands around my throat.

"What the fuck is wrong with you? Don't you ever throw something at me again! I will kill you, Diamond." He released his grip when he noticed he was hurting me.

I rubbed my neck that was now sore from his strength. I knew I was wrong for hitting him, but I was hurt. I was embarrassed and then I was pissed that he told me to step. I cried and he went into the bathroom to look at his head in the mirror, which had a small gash on it. I thought this was my cue to see if I could get into the bedroom. I eased off the couch and headed to the door. I tried to turn the knob but it was locked. I kicked it and immediately began screaming obscenities.

"Open the door, bitch! I know you're in there, you need to take your nasty ass to the clinic."

"Diamond, get the hell out." Davey came up behind me and pushed me from in front of the bedroom door. I could see the anger in his eyes. I had pissed him off, but he deserved it.

I decided not to fight anymore. I knew I would never see who was behind that door. I knew he would run to me later and tell me how sorry he was, but it didn't matter. He wasn't sorry now or any other time he'd said it. He probably didn't even know the meaning of the word. How could he? When you're truly sorry, you don't do it again. *Am I finally tired of his shit?* I asked myself. I didn't know the answer to that question and I probably never would.

I looked at him with tears still flowing freely from my eyes. I wanted to believe that there wasn't anyone in that room. I wanted to believe that today was just a nightmare and I would wake up in his arms. I wanted that old thing back. Instead we were here, fighting because he couldn't love me the way that I wanted him to.

I turned my back on him and headed to the living room. Exhausted, I grabbed my purse off the floor and headed out the door. I didn't even close it behind me. I got in the car and started it up. Looking up, I saw him standing there looking at me. *How did we get here?* I wondered. I'm sure he wondered the same thing. I backed out of the driveway and drove off. I wasn't in the mood to go home so I decided to go over to my girl Kiki's house.

Kiki had been my friend since the demise of my friendship with Mica. Kiki was older than me and had been through a lot. I could always go to her for a few words of wisdom. I sat in the car and tried to get myself together before going in. She hated to see me upset, so I didn't want her to know that I had been crying. She opened the door and immediately knew something was wrong.

"What the hell happened to your neck?"

"You wouldn't believe it, girl." Damn, I had forgotten about that. I couldn't even lie now if I wanted to. It was obvious I was choked since I had handprints around my neck. I stepped into her living room and headed for the sofa.

"Try me," she replied.

"I'm too embarrassed to even tell you." That was the honest truth. I didn't want anyone to know that I had an STD. I felt disgusting.

"Girl, you're like my baby sister. You can tell me anything."

I reluctantly gave up the tapes. "I had a doctor's appointment today and I found out that I have chlamydia."

"What? That dirty motherfucker. I told you to leave his ass alone."

"I went to his apartment and I know he had some bitch in there because he wouldn't let me get to the room. I wasn't leaving and then he had the nerve to tell me that if I wanted to step, then step. I lost it. I picked up one of his old basketball trophies and hit him right upside his damn head."

"He deserved that shit. I can't believe that he said that to you after all of the shit you've done for him."

"Then he fucking choked me. That's how I got these marks on my neck. He didn't hold on long. I can't even be mad that he choked me, though, because his head was bleeding on the side and shit." I laughed a little, trying to hide my pain. Because deep inside I wanted to cry and run back to him telling him I was sorry. Sorry for not being the woman that he wanted me to be. Sorry for not keeping him from straying away. I mean, some of it had to be blamed on me, right? If I was doing everything possible to keep him satisfied, he wouldn't be out fucking other people.

"I don't care if you hit his ass or not, he shouldn't have choked you. He's the one in the wrong here. Sometimes you have to hit a nigga upside the head so they can understand."

"Well, I don't think it made him understand anything. Shit, he still told me to get out after I tried to kick that damn bedroom door in."

"Fuck him, girl. You can't sit around and stress about a nigga like that. Yeah, he has money and I know that he spoils you, but what is that shit really worth? There are too many men like Davey out here."

"But I don't want another man. I want him to get his shit together," I said.

"Girl, you'll learn. You can't make a man be who you want them to be. If they aren't ready to settle down then there isn't anything you can do to change that. It's not your fault that he's a dog."

"So what should I do, just leave him alone?"

"Do what your heart says, baby girl. I can't tell you what to do but I will say this: Don't sit around being sad about the shit. Come out to the club tonight, have a good time, and let him come begging you. Not the other way around. If he really cares, he'll be back."

I sat there and took in what she said. I decided to take her advice and not call, begging him. I agreed to hang out at the club with her that night and in a way, I was excited. I hadn't been out in a while without Davey by my side. I wanted to try and have fun without worrying about chicks being all in his face. Though I had gotten used to it, it didn't make it any easier to deal with.

"So are you coming or what?" she asked, waving her hands in front of my face to break my daydream.

"Yes, I'm coming."

"Good, now take your ass to the store and get something for your neck. You can't come out to the club looking like someone gave you the death grip." She laughed.

I laughed too, though I didn't really find it all that funny. My relationship was in ruins and my man was with someone else. I left her house feeling a little better than I had before I got there. I went to the nearest Rite Aid to grab some cocoa butter for my neck and headed home to try and relax for a few hours before it was time to get ready for the club.

I got dressed that night in my little black dress, the kind that makes a man's mouth water. It hugged each of my God-given curves and was just tight enough at the butt to give me a Buffie the Body effect. My hair was down in a wrap with a Chinese bang. I had recently learned how to apply my makeup like a professional so I would definitely look like I was ready for a photo shoot. Davey was the last thing on my mind when I walked into the club called Solo, right on Columbus Boulevard—or if you're from Philly, you would call it Delaware Avenue. Kiki was a barmaid at the club so she always asked me to come down. Most times I would be with Davey but today I was rolling alone and it didn't bother me one bit.

As I headed inside I got tons of looks from both men and women. They probably wondered why the hell I was there alone. I could see the whispers and funny looks from the women. I tried my best to ignore them as I headed to the bar to find Kiki. Once I spotted her I headed over and waited until she got finished serving her customer.

"Hey girl, I'm glad you came out." She reached over the bar to give me a hug.

"Me too. I feel a little weird now that I'm getting a bunch of stares."

"Fuck them, girl. Enjoy yourself. What you drinking tonight?"

"Give me Hypnotiq and pineapple juice," I replied as I took a seat on the bar stool. It was still early so the club wasn't packed yet. After I got my drink I sat there and sipped it while scoping out the club. I was enjoying the music and feeling a buzz from the liquor. Soon, I was up out of my seat, dancing to the music. I didn't care that I was alone and my confidence must have been showing because the men were all over me.

After a couple hours of dancing I headed up to the bathroom. I hadn't even drunk that much, but I felt like my bladder was about to explode. As I was fixing my clothes, two girls walked in and as one went into a free stall, the other one stood on the outside and talked to her.

"Girl, I know you were cracking up inside that room," the one inside the stall said.

"That bitch was determined to get in there. I only stayed in there because Davey told me to."

Instantly I stood still. Was this the trifling bitch that gave him chlamydia? I became enraged.

"Davey is crazy. I'm glad he kicked her ass out of there. He knows you two belong together."

I couldn't take it anymore. I finished fixing my clothing and without a second thought burst out of the bathroom stall. She stood back when the door flew open, shocked. I didn't waste any time jumping on her. She fell to the floor from my weight and adrenaline combination. I began punching her, not giving her a chance to fight back. I grabbed hands full of her hair and began banging her head against the tile floor. Soon, there was blood coming from it. Her friend came from the stall, trying to jump on my back, but the bathroom attendant had already gotten security, who had come in just in time to pull her away. They grabbed me and as they pulled me away I gave her a couple of kicks. I continued to scream obscenities as they dragged me out of the club. Kiki noticed the commotion and ran from behind the bar.

"What the hell happened?"

"The bitch from the apartment was in there. I couldn't let that shit slide, Kiki. I just couldn't," I admitted.

The security guards held on to me until the cops arrived and handcuffed me. *What the hell did I get myself into now? Now* I wasn't using my head.

The cops took me down to the 26th police district and put me in a holding cell. After all that I had been through that day the only person I could think to call was Davey. When I was allowed to make a call, I dialed his number. I was nervous as I waited for him to pick up.

"Hello," his deep tone boomed through the receiver.

"Davey?"

"Diamond?"

"Yeah, I'm locked up. I need you to come and get me."

"Locked up?"

"Yeah, I saw that girl, Davey, and I couldn't help it. I wasn't thinking."

"That's why she's been blowing my phone up. Diamond, I can't believe you."

"Could you just please come and get me? I don't have anybody else to come."

"All right, I'll be there."

I knew he would be upset about my actions, but I also knew he loved me and wouldn't just hang me out to dry over a fling. Out of all the other incidents we'd had where another woman was involved, I never felt threatened until now. I always knew that they were just temporary and he'd drop them soon enough. This time was different, and it wasn't until now that I realized what my feelings for him truly meant. If I'd lost him, I wouldn't know what to do. I still felt bad about being there. I wasn't a criminal; I didn't belong there. I was simply a woman, crazy in love. Davey was mine and I wasn't going down without a fight.

I sat in the cell determined to make things better between the two of us. I knew that there were just some things that I was going to have to deal with. Today was the first time that he'd ever told me to leave, and I wanted it to be the last. I didn't want to lose him and whatever I had to do to keep him around, I planned on doing it.

Chapter Four

Mica: Role-Play

I lay stretched out across the bed trying to get some sleep. The day had been pretty long and I wanted to clear my head. I didn't know where the hell Tyson was but I never knew where he was. His business was always kept separate from me and I actually liked it that way. I knew that there would be things that I didn't like about it so I felt it was best that I knew nothing. We had been going strong for the past three months and I could admit that I never even wondered what he did when he wasn't around. The bottom line was that he always took care of me; he even kept my mom's bills paid, so I couldn't complain.

After a few minutes of tossing and turning I was asleep. Soon, I was awakened by a whisper in my ear. "Don't move," the male tone spoke lowly.

I didn't move as he removed the sheets, exposing my naked body underneath. I wanted to turn around to make sure that this was Tyson, but I knew if I did it would ruin the fun. The object of the game was to make the scene seem as real as possible, even though we both knew that it wasn't.

I loved changing roles; it kept our relationship spicy. The way I figured it is that most women lose their men when they are afraid to step out of the box and try something different. I wouldn't say I was a freak, but I did enjoy freaky things. I was pretty much down for anything and if giving him the feeling of being with someone different every night was what I had to do, I would do it. Don't get me wrong, I needed to be satisfied, and my man would do whatever he had to for me as well.

We didn't care what other people thought. Our rules were our rules and whatever happened outside stayed outside. I kept my eyes closed and my mouth shut as I had been directed to. I had butterflies in my stomach that were going crazy as his soft hands began to examine my body. He slowly massaged my back and caressed my ass as if I were a steak being prepped for a flavor rub. His tongue was wet and warm in the small of my back. The tickle of it sliding in between my cheeks was sending me wild. I tucked my head deep into the pillow trying not to make too much noise. I didn't want him to stop and I knew he would if he thought I was enjoying it too much. It was my duty to stay in character to make it enjoyable. So there I was, naked with my ass facing him. He continued to plant wet kisses all over my back before turning me over. The room was darker than it was when I fell asleep. I hadn't looked at the clock so I didn't have any idea of what time it was. I really didn't care about the time anyway. I wanted to make this last as long as possible.

Next, he took my hands and tied them to the headboard of the bed. I pretended to struggle a little. He was wearing a mask so I still couldn't see his face.

"Please, let me go," I begged, continuing to play the woman in distress.

"Shut up if you want to make it out of this alive."

I obeyed and didn't say another word. He stood up, staring at me for what felt like an hour before he began to fondle my breasts. My nipples hardened as he licked his fingers and rubbed them one by one.

"I'm gonna fuck the shit out of your fine ass."

I loved the sound of those words mixed with his deep voice. I wanted to be fucked. Hell, I needed it. I wanted to feel good tonight. With force he turned me over, tied my hands to the bedposts, and spread my legs almost to the limit. His fingers were tickling my legs—up and down he went as I squirmed, trying to free my hands from the top of the bed. I wasn't blindfolded but the room was dark and my eyes were closed. I would peek every now and then to see what he was doing. I could hear the zipper on his pants going down, which excited me. I was anticipating feeling him deep inside of me. He used two of his thick fingers to massage my wet clit. I almost came all over his fingers but he moved them just in time.

The next thing I felt was the head of his dick rubbing up and down my wet mound. He would slide the head in and then pull it back out to continue massaging me. After awhile I started rocking my hips to make more friction on the spot that I wanted him to hit.

He still was quiet but I found it extremely hard to hold in my moans. I was on my way to ecstasy and I didn't want to make any pit stops along the way. Soon, he had my legs resting on his strong shoulders. His dick was moving in and out of me for what seemed like an eternity. He was going like the Energizer bunny and I was enjoying every minute of it. I could hear him panting as if he was leading up to an orgasm. I rocked my hips harder to make sure that I came first.

My legs began to shiver as I erupted all over him. The loud moans that escaped my mouth sent him into his release. He was shaking as I wrapped my legs tighter around his neck. He didn't waste time getting up and releasing my hands. Before I knew it he was out of the room like a bandit and I was on my way back to sleep.

He never came home that night, but I wasn't mad since he had hit me off earlier. It wasn't as if he came home every night so I was never surprised when he didn't. The next morning I got up and showered. I had to meet my mom to take her out for lunch. Once a week I made it my business to spend time with her. I got to her house around eleven AM and we headed down City Line Avenue to go to Tequila's, the best Mexican restaurant in the city. I had a thing for Mexican food and I didn't know why. It wasn't like I'd hung around Mexicans or anything.

After we were seated I took the opportunity to break the ice. I always had to break the ice when talking to my mom because she was the type that wouldn't say anything unless you said something to her first.

"So, Mom, have you been out on any dates lately?"

"Dates? Girl, I'm forty-five years old. What the hell would I look like on a date?"

"What does your age have to do with anything? Nobody needs to be lonely." I stared at her, trying to figure out what the logic was in that. I don't give a damn if you're seventy, you're still entitled to have fun.

"A lot. Grown women don't date casually like young ones do. By the time you get my age you are supposed to be married with kids in college and settled down."

"Well, Mom, things didn't work out like that for you, so it's time to try something else. When was the last time you had sex?"

"Excuse me, I don't believe that's any of your business," she replied, annoyed by my line of questioning.

"Why not? I am your daughter so I believe that I have the right to be concerned. Maybe if you had a man you'd be happier."

"Who said that I wasn't happy? Having a man is definitely not the answer to all of your problems. If you ask me, they tend to make things worse."

"That's possible, but not all men are evil. Take Tyson, for instance, he's a good man. He even breaks his back to make sure that your bills are taken care of. It takes a special kind of man to do that."

"Well, maybe he's an exception to the rule,

Mica. It doesn't mean that I should jump on the first thing smoking hoping things will be better. I can do bad all by myself."

It was like talking to a brick wall when it came to my mom. Sometimes I felt like I was the mom and she was the daughter. Why was I trying to give a forty-five-year-old advice on how to get a man? Shit, by the time you're that age you should be a professional. I knew my dad was all she knew for years, but he'd been dead long enough for her to move on. It wasn't like he was going to come back from the dead or something and be pissed because she was dating. It didn't make any sense to me. My mom was good-looking for her age. She always dressed fly and she still had a shape. Most women get older and let themselves go. She always kept it tight; that's why my dad stayed around as long as he did. I got tired of trying to convince her that there was so much more out there for her to do. I decided not to continue the conversation and instead glanced at the menu to decide what I wanted to order before the waitress came back.

My mother sat across from me trying to avoid making eye contact. I definitely wasn't trying to upset her. I was merely trying to open her eyes.

"Are you mad?" I asked, trying to break the ice.

"Mad about what, Mica? Most of you young women think that you know it all. It's easier to imagine a perfect world than to live with reality. I've heard it all, seen it all, and been through it all. It's nothing that you're doing that I haven't done in the past. You may think that everything is gravy now because you're living the luxurious lifestyle, but my suggestion is that you hold onto some of that money so that when he's gone you'll be able to make it on your own."

"Tyson ain't going nowhere, Mom. Me and him got something different and ain't nobody gonna break us apart."

"Well, it doesn't have to be a person."

I give up. I wasn't going to sit there and keep trying to convince her. As soon as I saw the waitress I flagged her down. I was ready to get my food, hurry up and eat, and then take my black ass home. I would remind myself never to bring up men around her again.

The food came pretty quick and we sat quiet pretty much the whole time we ate. We both obviously had annoyed each other. We were out of the restaurant in record time. I couldn't wait to get far away from her. I know most would say that I was a fool for not listening to what my mother was saying, but I was happy with my life and my man. I know you are supposed to get wiser with age, but things had been too perfect for me to believe anything different. There had to be something said for a man who could make me smile just by the thought of his name. I had never loved anyone in the capacity that I loved him. I wanted the title, and he gave it to me, so my job was to keep playing the role that I longed to keep.

Chapter Five

Diamond: Him, Me, and She

"Babe, hurry up, we're going to be late!" Davey screamed through the apartment. I didn't understand what all the rush was about; he acted like we were late for something important.

"You act like this is so important, Davey. We're only going to have sex," I replied. As much as I hated to say it, it was the truth. Davey had bugged me for months to have a threesome. I wasn't interested in it, but I knew that I had to do whatever he wanted to keep him around. I figured that this was his way to cheat without me flipping out.

"It is important to me, and if making me happy is what you want to do, then it should be just as important to you as it is to me."

I still wasn't convinced and I really hoped he would change his mind and not make me go through it. "You know that I want to make you happy, I just don't understand why I have to do this."

"You always wondering why I cheat, that's why. You don't ever want to try new things and then you're pissed when I go get it from somewhere else."

"Davey, that doesn't have shit to do with it. You get it from somewhere else because that's what dogs do. Stop trying to blame all your fuckups on me."

"Babe, can we just go? This is turning into an argument for no reason. I just want to try something different with you and you told me that you were going to do it for me."

I reluctantly agreed to go because I didn't feel like arguing anymore. What was the point? He would do whatever he wanted to whether I went through with it or not. The entire car ride I was quiet. I didn't even know what to say. I just hoped that once this was over I would never have to do this again. I was nervous once we exited the car and headed to her apartment door. *What the hell was I doing?* I thought. I had never been interested in women, now here I was about to have sex with one all for the love of a cheating man. There was a time when I really believed that he loved me, but now I felt like he just used me to show off. He made sure that wherever we went everyone knew that I belonged to him. Shit, I couldn't even remember the last time that he told me that he loved me. I longed for that and for some strange reason I thought that the longer I kept doing what he needed me to do, he'd care about me the way he used to.

So, there we were sitting in her living room drinking whatever the hell she'd concocted. The more liquor I consumed the more comfortable I was with the surroundings. Nyssa was her name, and by the way the two of them conversed I knew that they had known each other for a while. She was a beautiful woman and just like me she'd probably been dragged into this by him. I wondered if she thought I was just a jump-off or if she really knew our history. I wasn't going to ruin the night by asking too many questions. Besides, I was feeling a buzz from the alcohol I had consumed.

I stared at her and registered everything about her in my mind. She had her hair wrapped with a Chinese bang sort of like mine. I didn't know if it was a weave or not because if it was, they did a damn good job putting it in. Her eyes were slanted a little, which made the hairstyle look even cuter. Her lips were perfectly covered with M•A•C Viva Glam V. (You knew you spent too much time in the store when you knew each number and color.) The neutral pink in the lip gloss was accentuated by the pink and black bustier she wore with the panties to match. When she opened the door with just her underwear on I was shocked at first and I don't know why, since I was well aware of what we came here to do.

"So, how are you feeling, Diamond?" she asked, with her legs crossed and her shoe hanging off of her foot.

"I'm feeling good. I don't know what you put in these drinks but they have me on cloud nine," I admitted.

"That's good." She set her glass down on the table and stood up from the sofa. "So, that means you're ready to get busy?" she asked.

"Yes," I agreed because at that point I had made up my mind—I was going to enjoy everything that they were going to give me tonight. Hell, if I was going to go through with it, I might as well get some satisfaction out of it. The worst thing I figured that could happen was that I'd enjoy it too much.

Soon, Davey was all over me as Nyssa instructed his every move. I thought it was strange that she was taking control of the situation but obviously it was her nature. I just tried to keep myself relaxed and go with the flow.

"Kiss her neck, she'll love that!" she spoke as she began to strip off her clothes. He softly kissed my neck as I became moist downtown. He took my ear into his mouth and sucked it, slowly letting it slip. He hadn't even touched my pussy yet and I was about to explode. The smell of his cologne was flowing up my nose and loosening me up even more. I was now even more relaxed and ready for whatever was approaching next.

He continued to kiss my neck as Nyssa sat in the chair on the opposite side of the room, watching. I was definitely turned on and wished that I had thought about having a ménage à trois a long time ago. His hands slowly found their way under my dress and as he pulled my panties to the side I released a loud sigh. I opened my eyes long enough to glance at Nyssa, who was smiling from ear to ear. She was obviously enjoying the show. I quickly shut my eyes again after he began to slowly massage my clit. With his free hand placed gently around my neck he removed his finger from my wetness and instructed me to taste it. I stuck out my tongue to lick my juices from his finger.

"Do you like that?" Nyssa asked.

"Yes!" I replied, trying to stay focused on Davey, who was now sliding his finger inside of my juicy tunnel. *Damn,* I thought to myself, *if this is only the beginning I can't imagine what the rest will be like.* His thick fingers continued to move in and out of me as I practically begged for more.

Nyssa stood up from the chair and made her way over to the sofa and began to unzip his pants to release his stiff rod. At that point I was like, *Okay, she's about to suck my man's dick. Is this the point where I stop it or is this the part when things get heated?* I didn't stop it. Instead, I closed my eyes again and continued to enjoy the pleasure and attention Davey was giving me. She slowly licked the head of his dick, taking in the pre-cum on the top. Within seconds she was deep-throating his stick and the sounds of it were exciting me even more.

"Do you want to taste this dick?" she asked as she glanced up at me.

I quickly responded, "Yes!" since I was eager to wrap my lips around the beautiful masterpiece. He stood up to remove his pants completely before sitting back down, and I got in position on my knees in front of him. Nyssa climbed up on top of the sofa so that her pussy was staring him in the face. I was soon sucking his dick like an ice-cold Popsicle and loving every second of it. Nyssa held her position up top, grinding her pussy into his face and moaning loudly. Soon his dick began to throb and the taste of his release was satisfying my taste buds and trickling down my throat. Nyssa got down off the sofa and instructed me to stop.

"Climb up top so he can suck that pussy, baby!" Before I moved forward she grabbed me to plant a sensual kiss on my lips. *Okay, before tonight that would have definitely made me uncomfortable.* She smacked me on the ass before nudging me to move forward. I climbed up on the couch and got in the same position that she had just been in. As soon as his tongue made contact with my clit I exploded and my juices poured out and ran down his chin. I tried to move away because the orgasm was causing me to tremble, but he quickly grabbed hold of my ass and pulled me back down. Soon I was riding his face like a trained jockey and he was sucking me like a lollipop.

Nyssa continued to suck his manhood while reaching up to insert one finger in my ass. As I moved back and forth on his face her finger moved in and out of my ass, which was more enjoyable than I could have ever imagined. As I neared another orgasm I bent over to grab hold of the back of the sofa and as I began to shake uncontrollably, I squeezed the plush leather.

"Come down and sit on this hard dick!" Davey spoke aloud. I was already exhausted but definitely anticipating feeling him inside of me. This was by far the best sex that I'd ever had. He pulled me close to him to kiss me. This was the most attention that he'd paid to me in months. His lips were soft and instantly put me at ease. He instructed me to get on my knees in front on the sofa while Nyssa sat down and opened her legs wide so that I could kiss her wetness. *Okay, what was I supposed to do now?* Eating pussy was definitely not something I knew how to do. I had seen it done in porno movies but had never stared a pussy in the face.

Davey slowly and deliberately entered me from behind as she palmed the back of my head to force my face deeper into her burrow. His dick filled me up completely and hit my G-spot continuously. Davey held on to my hips like a set of handlebars and picked up the speed. I forcefully sucked Nyssa's clit until she erupted, screaming loudly with delight. With the expression on her face, I figured that I had done the job right. Davey continued pounding me until we both came in sync. We were all exhausted as we relaxed. After I went to the bathroom and cleaned myself up, I waited patiently on the sofa for Davey.

"You ready to go?" he asked, as he headed back out to the living room, now fully dressed.

"Yeah, I'm ready," I replied, as I got up from the sofa and headed to the door. Nyssa walked over and opened the door for us.

"I'll talk to you later," Davey told her before giving her a hug.

"Thanks for coming, Diamond. I enjoyed myself. I hope that you did too." She reached over and gave me a hug as well. With that, we left her apartment and walked to the car. Again, I sat quietly in the car. I still didn't know what to say. I didn't really want to talk about how I just saw another woman suck his dick or him eating her pussy or me eating her pussy, for that matter. I just wanted to get home and go to bed. I hoped that this was enough for him to see that I was there for him and I was the woman that he needed to be with. I guess that he knew that I didn't want to talk about it, because he didn't say anything. He just kept his eye on the road and glanced over at me every so often. He softly held on to my hand with his right hand and drove with his left. *Was this a sign that we would grow closer again?* At least, I prayed that it was. I needed to be happy.

That night Davey lay next to me, snuggled up closely, and told me how much he loved me. I had my man back and I was planning on holding on to him.

Chapter Six

Mica: Three-Letter Word

I always wondered how a word so short could cause so much havoc. Just when you think things are going your way, *sex* comes into play and ruins it all. I wasn't an expert at how to handle relationship issues or infidelity, but I was soon about to learn. I knew that Tyson probably fooled around on me. I mean, what drug dealer doesn't have many women to choose from? What I didn't expect was to have to see it with my own eyes and figure out how to deal with it. No one really thinks about what they'll do if placed in certain situations, but we always hope that we will come out of them okay.

Tyson picked me up from the salon and told me that he had to make a stop before dropping me off at home. I hoped that it had nothing to do with drugs since he knew how I felt about that. I wanted to be as far away from that side of him as I possibly could.

Anyway, he pulled in front of a house off a small street and told me to wait in the car. He left the car running and told me that he'd only be a minute. Of course, I believed him and though I wasn't comfortable about being out there in the car alone, I agreed. I was becoming more annoyed as the seconds passed. I had been out there for at least a half hour, and he'd left his phone in the car so I couldn't even call him. I wondered what the hell was taking so long. After another ten minutes I was pissed.

I grabbed the gun he kept in the armrest of his car and put in inside my bag. After all, I didn't know what the hell I would run into once I got out. It was getting dark outside and I wasn't familiar with anyone or anything around there. The block was pretty much empty besides a few corner hustlers hanging in the Chinese restaurant at the end of the block. I was nervous as I exited but put on the persona that I wasn't. I knocked on the door a few times and waited, tapping my foot on the ground, hoping they would hurry up and open the door. A few seconds later a tall, thin-framed woman opened the door, tying her robe, which barely covered her naked body underneath. She was hazelnut in color and her hair was short and spiked. Her round breasts were practically hanging out of the robe. On looks alone I'd give her about a seven out of ten. Now, I considered myself a ten, so she was creeping up on me and that alone made me nervous.

"Can I help you?" she asked, stuffing her breasts into the robe, making sure they were covered.

"Yes you can. You can tell my man to get out here because I'm ready to go," I said, annoyed and wondering what the hell was going on inside the house.

"Well, he's a little busy right now, sweetie, so you're gonna have to go wait in the car until he gets finished." She looked me up and down as if I was two feet tall.

Sweetie? I wanted to slap her for trying to play me. I didn't think I looked that stupid.

"No, what you're going to do is go get him and tell him to come now," I raised my voice. I was getting angrier by the second.

"What I am going to do is close my door and finish what I was doing. I suggest you head back to the car like a good girl and wait for him to come out." She pointed her finger in my face almost close enough to touch me.

What the fuck was going on in there that would make her talk to me as if I were some groupie? I was fed up with talking to her. I quickly pushed her, making her stumble a little and pushed the door open. She began charging toward me but stopped when I took the gun out of my bag and pointed it at her.

"Back the fuck up, bitch! Now, where the fuck is my man?" I yelled.

She was backing away now and all of the mouth she had before disappeared. "What, are you going to do, shoot me?"

"Don't tempt me." I heard footsteps coming toward the steps. I hoped it was Tyson so we could just leave. I wasn't trying to go to jail, but if this bitch said one more word I was definitely going to shoot.

"Mica, what the fuck are you doing?" Tyson now stood at the bottom of the steps a few inches away from where Miss Smart-ass was standing.

"What the fuck are *you* doing? You had me sitting out in the car while you're in here fucking this bitch?"

"Mica, come on now. Why the fuck would I do some shit like that? Do you think I'm that crazy?"

"I think you're disrespectful, leaving me in that damn car and coming in here with her."

"She's such a fucking crybaby, Tyson. Why don't you get her the fuck out of my house?" she yelled, trying to hide behind him.

"You're still talking?" I asked, turning the gun in her direction.

"Mica, let's just leave and I'll explain everything to you in the car," he pleaded.

I really wasn't trying to hear much of what he was saying. I was standing there looking at them both, wondering how the hell my feelings for a man could make me go crazy enough to pull out a gun. I didn't want to believe that it was just him, but instead, that it was the disrespect that the female standing across from me showed. I didn't take to that sort of thing kindly.

"I'm going to leave, but you can stay here with this bitch. I'll call a cab." I tossed his gun to him and turned my back to head out of the door.

"Mica, I'm not letting you leave me. This house is where they bag up the drugs, okay? I'm not here fucking anybody. If you don't believe me I'll show you."

I turned back around and looked at him, and then I glanced at her while she stood there with a

smirk on her face. I wanted to sma
of her. Even if he was telling the truth
her nor did I like the way she talked to
came to the door. In my mind I was thinki
didn't really want to see what was upstairs, ..in
my heart I had to know if he was lying.

"Yeah, I need to see it," I said, walking toward
him.

He walked up the steps and told me to follow
him. I was nervous as I headed up behind him. I
wanted to just say stop. I mean, if he had gone this
far it had to be true. I didn't want to see anything
that would put me in a difficult situation had he
ever gotten caught. I couldn't tell anything that I
didn't know, but knowing and keeping it a secret
would probably tear me apart.

"Tyson, I don't need to go any farther. I believe
you, okay?"

"Are you sure? I don't want to hear about this
later when I have to stop by here again."

"I'm sure. Let's just go, okay?" I said as he
turned around on the stairs and began to walk
back down. We left the house and got into the car.
I was glad that I didn't go any farther but I was
pissed that I acted the way that I had. I felt embarrassed. I never wanted anyone to see me in such a
vulnerable position. I was almost ready to go to
jail rather than lose him to someone else. It was almost as if another person was taking over my
body because in the past I would have never let a
man get the best of me.

Once we reached his house I felt like a load had
been lifted off of me. Not because of the argument, but because he was telling the truth. I still

...cn't believe that he never cheated on me, but at least he didn't that night. Most women would say that I was a fool, and in some instances I would probably agree. Though I may be a fool in love, I was well taken care of for all of the drama I had to deal with. I loved Tyson more than anyone else that had come my way and for good reason. I had never met a man that could walk into a room and command everyone's attention without saying a word. He was the type everyone fell in love with. He kept you smiling and he never acted like he was better than anyone else or as if his shit didn't stink. He was smart and actually had a college degree. Now how many hustlers can say that? I was proud of my man and happy to be his woman.

Once we entered his house he headed straight to the living room and turned on CNN. He loved to be up on the news. He knew what was going on in every state from shootings to the weekly weather. This was the time that he didn't like to be bothered and most of the time I would respect that, but tonight I wanted to give him an apology that he could feel. I couldn't deal with the silent treatment and knew that I had to do something to get back on his good side.

I headed upstairs and took a shower. After my shower I lotioned up with my favorite Bath & Body Works scent. I put on the matching body splash and slipped on a bra and thong with a garter belt and stiletto heels. I put my hair in a little bun and took a deep breath. I hoped that he wouldn't turn me away—I mean, he had never done it before, but tonight I had acted out of the ordinary so there was a possibility that he would.

I slowly walked down the steps and due to the plush carpet you couldn't hear the sounds of the shoes. I crept into the living room hoping that he wouldn't turn around before I got close enough to him. I wanted to surprise him.

I decided that I would get close to him and sing into his ear. I needed it to be freaky and with the voice that I had been blessed with I knew he wouldn't be able to turn me away. I settled on "Nasty Grind" by Adina Howard. I loved the sex-filled songs and I had always wanted to perform for him.

I walked toward the back of the sofa and slowly put my hands on his shoulders. He didn't budge but he didn't push my hands away either, which was a plus and my cue to keep going. I bent down so that I could get close to his ear. I started the song and hoped that he would receive it the way that I wanted him to.

By now I was standing in front of him dancing to the words that I was singing. He had used the remote to turn off the TV, which excited me because now I had his full attention. I continued singing and watching his expressions. I wanted to jump right on him, but I continued the performance to make it sensual.

I moved closer to the sofa and placed one leg at a time onto the seat so that he could remove my shoes. Next, I took off my bra, letting my perfect double D's loose. I slowly bent over so that my breasts were in his face. He didn't waste any time grabbing hold of them and caressing my hardened nipples. I moaned as I got more excited. I wanted to feel his lips all over my body and let him know when he missed a spot. I straddled him as he held

his position on the sofa. I met his lips with a deep
kiss and massaged his tongue with mine. I can
hardly explain how good I felt at that moment. I
felt like I was intoxicated with love and he was the
designated driver. My insides were going wild as
he used one hand to massage my clit through my
black lace panties.

"You want this pussy?" I moaned in the sexiest
tone. He didn't respond so I pulled back enough to
release my nipple from his mouth and asked
again, "Do you want this pussy?"

"More than you know," he responded in his sexy
baritone voice.

I rose up and began to unbuckle his pants to release his hard dick. I was as anxious to wrap my
lips around it as I would be to eat my last meal. I
looked up at him just so that our eyes could meet
one last time before I went to work. He gave me a
slight smile and then he gently put his head back,
anticipating what I was about to give him.

Even after a year of us being together we managed to still turn each other on as if it were something new. That was definitely something special,
because not many couples can achieve that.

His dick was hard as a brick as I took one lick of
the head and used my finger to wipe the pre-cum
across my lips. He loved when I did the freaky shit
and I loved turning him on. I wrapped my lips
around the head and slowly sucked from top to
bottom. I made sure that his shaft was soaking
wet so that the slurping sounds would keep him
excited. I had gotten really good at giving head; so
much so that I didn't even have to think about it. I
would go straight to work on it.

After ten minutes or so of foreplay I was ready to feel him inside of me. I stood up, releasing my grip on his dick, watching it stand on its own at attention. I slid my thong off and let them hit the floor. I straddled him with my back facing him and began going up and down, filling my wet pussy with his huge dick. I was moaning and rubbing my breasts. He was moaning with me, almost in sync. My ass was slapping so hard against him you could have heard it upstairs. I wanted to cum but I wanted us to do it together so I held onto it. I continued to rock my hips and swirl them as if I were trying not to drop a hula hoop. He reached his hands around and played with my clit, which made it extremely hard to hold onto my eruption.

Tyson held onto me and stood up, making sure that his dick didn't slip out of me. I placed my hands on the arm of the sofa as he began to pound me from behind. I was throwing my ass back hard, trying to show him that this pussy was his. I felt my orgasm building and I couldn't stop it because that shit felt way too good.

"Oh shit, I'm about to cum," I moaned.

He grabbed hold of my hips and began pumping faster. He was moaning loudly, letting me know that he was about to cum as well. My legs began to shake and soon my juices were splashing all over him. Within seconds of my release his fluid was pouring out inside of me.

I felt relaxed and I was glad that we had been able to get past the events that took place earlier in the evening. No woman should be able to take me out of my square or threaten to ruin my relationship. I was paying close attention now, and I knew exactly what I had to do to keep from losing my cool again. The three-letter word, *sex*, was no longer a factor. I wasn't going to assume anymore. I had to believe that he wouldn't disrespect me and he'd keep the sideline hoes in check.

Chapter Seven

Diamond: As Seen on TV

Things had been going great for Davey and me in the months that followed. I had even moved back in with him into his apartment. Summer was coming and I was getting anxious because we had planned on taking a much-needed vacation. The episode with Nyssa was behind us and he hadn't mentioned it since the night that it went down. I never told anyone about it and I planned on keeping it a secret until the end of time. I didn't want anyone to think any less of me. I had managed to keep the fire lit between Davey and me but some things are too good to be true and some people are never satisfied.

Kiki called me one afternoon while I was doing some much needed cleaning around the apartment. I had been focusing on my relationship so much lately that I hadn't paid anything else much attention. Had I known what I was about to hear I would have sat down before she spoke, but I didn't and damn near hit the floor in shock.

"Diamond, I got some shit to tell you, girl!"

"About what? You know I'm always up for hearing some gossip," I admitted.

"It's about you and that trifling-ass nigga you're with."

"What have you heard now? People always trying to throw salt in the game when they see we're doing fine."

"Girl, I didn't hear it, I saw it for myself. You know that nigga is going around selling a sex tape of you and him having a threesome!"

"What?" I asked, because I wanted to make sure that I heard it right. Would he really do that to me? I couldn't believe my ears.

"Yes, girl. I didn't know you went both ways, girl. That shit looked like a professional production." She laughed.

I didn't find anything funny about it. There I was doing what I needed to do to satisfy my man and he secretly taped the scene and made money from it. I knew she wasn't lying about seeing it. How else would she have known that I'd had the threesome and actually had sex with a female?

"I don't go both ways and I did that shit for him and this is how he repays me?" I couldn't hold back the tears. I was so embarrassed that something I was so uncomfortable about doing was being spread around like government cheese. The whole world was seeing me in that vulnerable position.

"Girl, I don't know why you are still with his ass.

When are you going to wake up and smell the coffee?"

"I'm going to have to talk to you later, Kiki. I have to finish cleaning." I quickly cut her off and ended the conversation. I was furious. With Davey, there was always something. I thought that we had made it past the bullshit and here was another slap in the face. I couldn't answer her question because I didn't know. I didn't know when I would wake up and smell the coffee. I didn't know when I was going to realize that he wasn't shit. I didn't know how many times I had to be hurt by him before I decided to walk away.

I sat there crying for hours. I still had the broom in my hand when he came in. I was sitting on the sofa, still in disbelief. He immediately knew that something was wrong and before he got a chance to speak, I interrupted him.

"Just when I think that you've changed I get a slap in the face. I can't believe that you would sell a fucking sex tape of me that I didn't even agree to!" I yelled.

"What are you talking about?"

"You know what the fuck I'm talking about! I got a call today from someone telling me that you're out on the streets selling a sex tape of the threesome we had."

"I never sold a tape; I didn't even know that there *was* a tape!"

"You expect me to believe that shit, Davey! I can't fucking believe you would do this to me." I still sat there crying. I was just seconds away from jumping up, but I knew that hitting him wasn't going to solve anything. It surely wasn't going to get him to admit that he would degrade me this way.

"Diamond, Nyssa must be the one selling the tape. I didn't know anything about it, believe me."

"So, if I go to that bitch's house and kick her ass you'll still tell me that?"

"Diamond, you can't do that," he said, still holding his position near the front door.

"What the fuck do you mean I can't? You don't make the fucking rules! Why are you trying to protect her and I'm supposed to be your woman?"

"Diamond, my son will be there. You can't do that!"

"Your son? Since when did you have a son?" I had to ask that question because he never told me anything about having a child before. This was definitely a shock to me. Then I thought about it even deeper. So Nyssa was his baby's mother? What the fuck? I damn sure didn't sign up for this shit.

"He's three years old," he replied in a low tone, almost as if he was afraid to say it any louder.

"You mean to tell me you have a three-year-old son? So you fucking cheated on me and had a baby? And then had me fuck your baby's mother?" That was it; I couldn't sit still any longer. I got up from the chair and began hitting him with the broom. He tried to get ahold of it, but the wooden stick broke over his arm. Once it broke I moved closer and began punching him. After a few seconds he got ahold of my arms and held them. I tried kicking him once I couldn't get my hands free.

"You're lucky I don't have a gun because I'd

shoot your ass! Get the fuck off of my hands," I yelled, trying to get my hands free so that I could leave. I wasn't going to stay in this apartment any longer. I couldn't believe the twisted shit that he had gotten me involved in. He'd had a child and never told me. That hurt my heart because at one point I was pregnant by him and he forced me to get an abortion. I went along with it because I wasn't trying to raise a baby alone if he backed out on me. So, to hear this was like a stab in the heart. Then I thought back to the tape. *How many people have seen it?* I guess he felt like a fucking king having me and his baby's mom fucking him on tape.

"Get the fuck off of me," I continued to yell. Tears were pouring out of my eyes and I was like a raging bull trying to get lose. I bit and kicked him until he finally let me go.

"Diamond, I'm sorry that I didn't tell you, but I didn't want to hurt you."

"How the fuck did you think I would never know? I guess you didn't plan on being with me very long, huh? You can keep your apology because it's bullshit, just like this fucking relationship. I never meant shit to you. There is no way that you could love me and do the shit that you continue to do to me. I'm leaving, Davey, and don't bother calling me because you won't get an answer."

I turned and walked toward the bedroom to gather up a few things. Kiki told me that if I ever needed a place to crash that I could come stay with her. I was going to take her up on that because at that point this thing I thought was a relationship was officially over.

"Diamond, please, let's talk about this. Don't walk out on me like this."

"Fuck you. You are never going to do right by me and I'm not going to keep being your fool."

"We can fix this. I know I fucked up, but give me another chance to make it right."

"How many times have I heard that line? I'm done Davey," I replied as I grabbed my bag and headed back toward the door. I couldn't stand the sight of him. I felt sick to my stomach the longer the thoughts weighed on my mind. I would have never believed that he would stoop this low. I mean, how could you not tell me about a child? Three fucking years? I'd been a fool for way too long.

My heart felt like it had been shattered and my body was extremely weak. I could barely stop shaking long enough to control the steering wheel in the car. I made it over to Kiki's house safely, though I almost got in two accidents, being an emotional wreck. I was almost too embarrassed to knock on the door. I hadn't called and given her a heads-up, but she probably already expected that I would be coming after she told me about the tape. I knocked softly since I couldn't exert enough energy to use any force.

"Girl, I knew you were coming. I hope you're leaving his sorry ass for good!" She reached out and grabbed my shoulder to pull me inside. "You know you can stay here as long as you need to."

I was glad I had a friend like Kiki. I had some relatives, but since I found out I was adopted I never really felt like I belonged. I hadn't even seen my mother in months. I called from time to time to check on her, but I never made it down to the place that I once called home to actually see her. I had heard through the grapevine that she'd been using drugs. I knew I couldn't believe everything I heard, but once she and my dad broke up, she lost it. She gave up on herself, and living in North Philly surrounded by a bunch of drug dealers didn't help, either.

Once I got with Davey things changed. My family grew jealous of the things that he did for me. I strayed away from them and hadn't been back since. So, there I was clinging on to the only person who had been my friend since leaving my grandmom's house a few years back. I met Kiki while hanging out at the club with Davey. He was pretty well known and when he said that he wanted to show me to the world, that was exactly what he did. He didn't waste time showing his trophy off. Kiki, though cordial with him, never really cared for his type. She always told me that men like him aren't to be trusted. She warned me about falling in love, but by that time I had already fallen hard. I had smacked the ground hard and couldn't peel myself away from it.

Surprisingly, he allowed me to hang out with Kiki when he was working or when he wanted to get loose in the club. The women would be all over him and there were plenty of times that I almost came to blows with chicks for the blatant disrespect. Kiki always had my back but at the same time tried to diffuse any altercation. I respected her for that the more I learned that men will be men. She had been there for me every time I had a blow-out with Davey. Whether it was an ear to listen, a shoulder to lean on, or a place to lay my head until I decided to take him back, she was always there. For that I was grateful and I planned to repay her one of these days.

I took a long shower that night, damn near using all of her hot water. I let the water hit my face, hoping that it would drown my pain. The more I tried to think about him the harder it was. I pulled myself together and after the shower I went to bed in her extra bedroom. I closed my eyes and soon I was off in la-la land, praying that tomorrow would be a better day.

Chapter Eight

Mica: Family Matters

In my attempt to get close to Tyson I'd moved in with him. At first I wasn't all too keen on the idea, since I knew it would take time for him to get used to me being around all the time. I didn't want to impose on his daily routine, but I wanted to get closer to him.

A little over a month had passed since the day I burst in the stash house making a fool of myself and I had managed to stay on his good side ever since. Things were good but there's always drama and I knew there was someone waiting in the wings to throw salt in the game.

"Hello, is Tyson there?" a female voice boomed through the receiver.

I had to sit for a second before responding. I couldn't believe that a bitch would have the audacity to call here for him. I didn't know what to say so I said the first thing that came to mind.

"Excuse me?"

"I *said*, is Tyson home," the female replied, annoyed.

"Who is this?"

"None of your business. I just need to know where Tyson is."

"That's not an attitude that gets answers."

"Well, if you must know, this is Deanna, his son's mother."

"Well, Deanna, Tyson isn't here and I suggest the next time you speak with him you get his cell number."

"First of all, Little Miss Prissy, I was around long before you and I'm still going to be here when you're gone so you can talk that shit if you want, but you're going to end up with the broken heart."

"I'm not going anywhere, so if someone is going to end up with a broken heart it's going to be you."

"Why would I have a broken heart? If you don't know, I know Tyson like the back of my hand and he changes women like he changes his drawers. I'm the one who's got the baby and the title. Have you forgotten he married me, or did he not tell you that? He's got to divorce me to get rid of me, and even then I got his kid so he's bound to me for life."

"Is that why you called here? Does that make you feel better? Because honestly, I don't give a fuck about that. The bottom line is he's my man and I ain't going nowhere."

"Don't be so sure about that. Tyson doesn't give a fuck about you. You'll see. Now when he comes home, tell him I called and you make sure you have a good day."

Click.

I heard the sound of the dial tone before I could say another word. Tyson always told me how crazy his ex was, but one thing she didn't know was how crazy I could get. I tried to keep my cool but the bottom line is there wasn't but so much that I could take before I was fed up. I couldn't wait to talk to him to let him know about the conversation. It was about six o'clock when he walked in the door and I instantly began my case.

"You know that bitch called here disrespecting me? When are you going to put her in her place?" I yelled, walking toward the door, where he was still standing in the vestibule.

"What bitch? Who are you talking about, Mica?"

"Deanna. I wish you would put her in her place!"

"And where is that? She's a grown-ass woman. I can't tell her what to do."

"What the fuck do you mean you can't tell her what to do? So what you're saying is that it is okay for her to disrespect me?"

"That's not what I am saying, I'm saying that I can't do shit about her ways. That's just how she is, that's why we aren't together now."

"You might as well be with her, you won't divorce her." I was pissed. It was bad enough they were still married but he wouldn't even stand up for me. It wasn't rocket science. All he had to do was tell her that she had to stop calling here.

"You know what, Mica? The attitude ain't gonna make shit change. She knows that I'm with you and that's all that matters. I don't know what the fuck else you expect me to do."

"I don't want to hear shit when I have to fuck her up! Ain't nobody going to keep disrespecting me."

"It's not that deep. You're turning it into something else."

"How do you figure it's not that deep?"

"Look, would you just drop it? I'll talk to her, Okay? I got enough shit to deal with for y'all to keep arguing all the time. Satisfied now?"

"I'll be satisfied when she stops calling," I snapped before leaving the room.

I knew he probably wouldn't talk to her. I was tired of her feeling like she was in control. When things got serious with me and Tyson, he told me that she would never be an issue. It didn't take very long before I found out that was so far from the truth you couldn't reach it. I thought I could handle it but the longer it went on the more I realized I couldn't. I begged him on many occasions to stop giving her the number to the house, but his excuse was that she had to have it in case something happened to his son. I mean, his cell number should have been sufficient. I didn't think I was crazy, nor did I believe that it was too much to ask.

I headed upstairs to get my purse so I could leave. I needed some fresh air to calm me down. I started thinking of where I could go, and my thoughts about cousin Deidra, from my father's side of the family, popped up in my mind. I hadn't seen her in six months, and the last time I saw her it was so brief that I hadn't been able to find out what she'd been up to. I missed her. Deidra and I were pretty close growing up, but once my father passed we kind of strayed apart. Deidra's mom was one of the coolest moms on earth. She allowed Deidra to do things my mom wouldn't go for even now that I was an adult. I tried to hang out with her as much as possible. I felt like I was a student trying to suck up any information she could give me. I admit that I was always a bit envious of her, since she had boyfriends and all the fly clothes. The things that most teenagers dream of having, she had. She didn't have a curfew, whereas I had to be in when the streetlights came on.

My mother never really cared too much for my dad's family, but dealt with them because of him. After he was killed his family didn't want anything to do with us. They blamed my mother for his death. I never understood why they blamed her. I mean, Johnny was *his* child too.

I was tired of being cooped up in the house. I wanted to take a drive, which was something that I didn't usually do. I rarely drove anywhere, especially long distances. That was why I always caught the bus to see Johnny. I dialed Diedra's number from my cell phone but the number was disconnected. Since I didn't have any other number to reach her at I decided to just drive to her house and surprise her with a visit. I got on I-95 North toward Aramingo Avenue. I sat in the car bobbing my head to the sounds of Mary J. Blige. I loved her music. No matter what you were going through you could always find a song of hers that matched your situation. I found a parking spot and walked toward the entrance of the building. I noticed a guy named Money, who I hadn't seen in a while, standing on the corner.

"Money? Is that you?"

"Mica? What's up? What the hell you doing in this hood?" he asked before hugging me.

I had the biggest crush on Money while I was growing up. I was always the shy one in the bunch, so I never had the opportunity of telling him. By the time I gathered up the courage to tell him, he had already gotten with Deidra. I never told either one of them that I had the crush, so I couldn't blame anyone but myself.

"I came by to see Deidra. I haven't seen her in a while."

"A lot has probably changed since the last time you saw her."

"What do you mean by that?"

"I'm not going to throw no salt on her but she ain't the same ol' Deidra no more."

I didn't know what the hell he was talking about. I mean, how much could she have changed in six months? She looked perfectly fine to me before.

"I still don't get it, Money. What happened to her?"

"You'll see for yourself, but it's good seeing you, though. I see life's treating you good."

"Yeah, I'm doing good, found me a good man finally," I said, laughing.

"That's what's up, you deserve it. I'm not gonna hold you, though. Go see how your cousin is. I'll see you around."

"Okay, good seeing you," I replied, before heading toward her apartment. I climbed the two flights to get to her door. I knew I needed to exercise more because I was exhausted after that. Anyway, I knocked a few times before I heard the locks being turned. I was nervous to see who was behind it. The comment Money made was replaying in my mind like a skipping CD. Still, I stood there hoping that he was just exaggerating.

"Who the hell are you here for?" a thin-framed woman asked through a crack in the door, showing only her body. I couldn't see her face so I knew that she couldn't possibly see mine.

"I'm here to see Deidra."

"Who are you? What do you want with her?"

"I'm her cousin, Mica. I just want to see how she's—"

"Mica? Hey girl, where have you been?" The thin frame was that of Deidra. I didn't know what to say as she reached her arms out to hug me. I had never seen her so thin, and I wasn't sure if I even wanted to know what was going on with her. Instantly two things popped in my head: either she was on drugs, or she had HIV. The last time I saw her she looked perfectly healthy. It wasn't as if she had been a big woman, but her frame looked healthier than the emaciated look it had now.

"Come in, girl. I missed you," she said, motioning for me to come inside the apartment.

"You were on my mind so I tried to call you. The number was disconnected so I just stopped by." The apartment was a mess. Clothes and food containers were everywhere. I didn't even want to sit down for fear I would carry some unwanted rodents home with me.

"Yeah, I couldn't afford it, girl, so I had to let it get cut off. I see you dressed all fly. Life must be good for you."

"Yeah, it is. What's going on with you? I have never seen you this thin."

"I know, girl. To be honest, I got messed up on some shit. Hanging with the wrong people getting high, the drugs kept calling my name. I couldn't stop."

I was shocked that she just blurted that out. I'd never seen a drug addict who could be honest about their habits. "Deidra, how did this happen? You were doing so good the last time I saw you."

"I know, I'm embarrassed for you to even see me like this. Truthfully, the last time you saw me I was already hooked. I couldn't tell you that. You always looked up to me but now what do you have to look up to? I look like shit and I know it. The problem is that I don't know another way—this is all I know now." She couldn't even look me in the eye as she talked. What the hell happened to the strong woman I knew? She had the best of everything, clothes, money, and a man that most women would fight tooth and nail for.

"What happened to G? Last time I saw you y'all were on the way down the aisle."

"Girl, he left me for some skinny bitch that he knocked up. I was depressed for a long time, but the drugs helped ease my pain."

I still sat there as if the whole scene wasn't really happening. I hoped it was just a cruel joke and things were really okay. I couldn't believe what my eyes were seeing, and even if someone were to pinch me and *say wake up, this is real* I still would doubt it.

"Is there any way that I can help you? I hate seeing you like this." I was almost in tears. It hurt my heart to see her in such a vulnerable state.

"If you can lend me a few dollars that would

help me a lot." She still hadn't looked me in the eye yet.

I grabbed her by the chin to lift her head. "You know I can't do that, D. You won't use it for what you should. I want to help you out of this. If I find a rehab program for you, will you go?"

"Rehab? Hell no, I'm not going to no rehab."

"What's wrong with rehab? Is this the way you want to live? The woman I know would never turn down help."

"I'm not the woman you used to know, baby girl, a lot of shit has changed. I'm not happy like this, but who's to say that I'll be happy when I'm clean? Ain't shit out here for me."

"Yes there is, D, you just don't want to see it."

"I don't have nobody, no man, no family. Without love in my heart I might as well be dead. Nobody gives a fuck about me."

"I do," I replied as a tear fell from my eye. "Let me help you, please, I can't see you like this; it's hurting me, D."

"I'm sorry Mica, but I can't, okay? I appreciate the offer, I really do, but it's just not for me."

I grabbed my purse and took out a business card and fifty dollars. I didn't know what else to do. I gave her the card and told her to call me if she changed her mind or needed me for anything. I prayed that she would use the money wisely, but I knew that it would never happen. I didn't know many drug addicts, but I did know that they would lie, cheat, and steal to get high. I felt that at least she was honest and told me about her addiction. I gave her a hug and told her how much I loved her. I really did care about her and at that point, probably more that she cared about herself. I left her apartment saddened. I kind of wished that I had never stopped by. I know things happen for a reason, and maybe it was meant for me to see her to help her out. I wasn't going to give up on her that easily, but I wanted to give her some time to think. If there was one thing that mattered to me it was family and I was coming back for her whether she wanted me to or not.

That night I had the hardest time sleeping. I tossed and turned so much Tyson woke up and asked what was wrong. I broke down and told him about Deidra.

"When I left earlier I went to see my cousin Deidra, who I haven't seen in a while. I wasn't prepared for what I saw and it's eating me up inside."

"What do you mean, what you saw? What's wrong with her?"

"She's strung out—I mean she's so thin. This is a person I used to look up to. Back in the day she was the shit, she had the looks, the money, and the man. I was so jealous of her. She needs help and I feel like an asshole for walking out of there."

"Babe, you can't blame yourself for what's happening to her."

"I don't, but I shouldn't have left, I should have stayed. I'm all that she has." I began to cry. I honestly believed that I should have stayed even though she turned me down.

"Come here babe, you can't save everybody. I know that's your family and you love her, but if she's not ready to be helped nothing you say will change that. Hopefully she'll come around before it's too late." He wrapped his arms around me and wiped the tears from my face. I knew that what he said was true even though I didn't want to believe it. I wanted to believe that I could just walk in there and drag her to a rehab to get help. Unfortunately, that wasn't a reality. When she was ready I was sure she'd let me know. The best thing I could do now was let her know I was there for her and I loved her. At least if she had that to fall back on she would fight to get herself on track. I soon fell to sleep in Tyson's arms, forgetting about the brief argument we'd had earlier in the day. He'd always been good at consoling me, and right then I needed him more than ever.

Chapter Nine

Diamond: Running His Game

"If it isn't little Miss Diamond Diva. What the hell brings you to this part of town? I thought you were allergic to North Philly," Cicely said, standing back, looking me up and down. "Mom, you'll never believe what the wind blew in."

"Hey, Aunt Cicely, it's nice to see you too," I replied sarcastically. I wasn't really happy to see her. On the real, I never really liked her ass anyway. I only dealt with her because she was my mom's sister. I didn't know what made me stop by there, but once I saw her face I wanted to turn back around and leave. I made sure to press the alarm pad on my key ring again to make sure my car was locked before going inside. You could never be too careful in that neighborhood. I'd be pissed if I came out and my car was missing.

"Where's my mom at?" I asked, trying to get

straight to the point. I didn't want to stay there longer than I had to.

"Your mom? Who the hell knows where she is? Maybe you should try the local crack houses or speakeasies," Cicely replied, being the bitch that she normally was.

My grandmom stepped in. "Cut it out, Cicely. All of that isn't necessary."

I was about two seconds away from punching Cicely in the face, and my grandmom could probably sense that. There had been many times that she and I had come close to blows. I never knew if her anger came from jealousy or if she just hated me so much that she had to continuously push my buttons. I remember the day we moved in, she had to rub it in my mother's face how she knew she'd be back. My mother had been the only one of my grandmother's children who was successful, and Cicely, being the oldest, hated it.

"Why? It's the truth. She needs to know that her perfect mother ain't so perfect after all," she said, before leaving the room and heading toward the kitchen.

My grandmom came over to try and calm me down. "Don't let her rile you up, you know how she gets."

I was still pissed and it would take a lot more than a few words to put out the steam. "I don't know why she always has to be so negative. She acts like I did something to her."

"That's just her attitude. She's always mad at the world, but you can't let that stop you from doing what you came here to do."

"What's that?" I asked, confused. I only stopped by to see my mother, and since she wasn't there I was planning to be on my way. I didn't have anything else on the agenda but maybe she knew something that I didn't know.

"To save your mom. She really needs you. She's been so depressed and she uses those drugs to break away from reality. I tried everything that I could think of, but God has a strange way of working sometimes. Everything happens for a reason and it was meant for you to come here today whether you believe it or not."

I sat there listening to all she said and I was definitely a firm believer of things happening for a reason. Some things I just didn't know the answer to, and I guessed I would know when I was supposed to.

Just as Grandmom was wrapping up all that she had to say, the front door opened and my mother walked in. I hadn't seen her in months, and I almost didn't recognize her. Her hair was all over the place and her clothes were so big they were barely staying up on her small frame. She had lost so much weight and looked far different from the woman who raised me. What the hell happened? I mean, when I left her the last time she was doing well with a new job. She was excited that she was going to finally be able to make it on her own. I could barely stand to look at her. She glanced over at me but appeared to be so high that she didn't even know who I was.

"Mom, it's me, Diamond," I said, standing up from the chair that I had been sitting in and heading in her direction.

"Diamond? Girl, what brings you around here?" she asked before sitting down on the sofa on the opposite side of the large living room.

"I came to see you, to find out how you were doing. I wanted to see if you needed anything."

Her eyes lit up like the sun when I said that. I didn't know if that was good or bad. "Actually, baby, if you could help me out with a few dollars, I can go out and look for a job."

"What happened to the job you had?"

"I got fired, baby. I couldn't make it to work on time. It was so far away."

I knew she was lying, but I couldn't prove it so there wasn't any sense in arguing about it. "How much money do you need?" I asked, reaching into my bag to get my wallet.

"Just about fifty dollars. I can get me a TransPass and get my hair done up nice."

I knew she was lying but I wasn't going to tell her no. She had done far too much for me, and I couldn't stand to see her the way she was. My grandmom saw that I was about to give her money and looked at her with disgust as she headed out of the room. I pulled out one hundred dollars and gave it to her. She smiled and gave me a hug.

"Are you really going to look for a job, Mom?"

"I am, baby. I promise."

"I'm going to come back and check on you. I want you to get better, Mom, so things can be like they used to be."

"I know you do, and things will get better."

I took her word since I hoped that she would get better. I didn't know what else to do. I thought about moving her out of the neighborhood, but that wouldn't stop her from coming back if she wanted to. I even thought about offering to put her in a rehab, but one thing about a drug addict was that they wouldn't take the help if they weren't ready for it. I prayed that she would get better before it was too late.

After saying my good-byes I left feeling a little better that I had gotten to see my mom. There was nothing worse than hearing through the grapevine that your mother was on drugs, especially when you bailed out on her. I did believe that if I'd stayed around she may have never been steered the wrong way. Once I left I figured that she felt like she had no one to live for. Somehow I had to make her believe again, since I knew that I was the key to her getting better and I understood what my grandmom meant.

I had to meet Davey at five and I was running late. I hated being late because when I was in a rush everyone in the city was driving Miss Daisy. Davey claimed that there was something important I had to do for him. I didn't have a clue what it was, but I damn sure hoped that it wasn't another threesome. After the sex-tape incident I knew that I should have just up and left, but it was something about him that made me stay. It took the last four months to shake the visions of that night. I definitely wasn't trying to go there again.

So what made me love him? I couldn't pinpoint it, and even if I could no one would understand it anyway. There are a lot of relationships that don't make sense to us from the outside looking in. I was on the inside and I couldn't see my life any other way. So again I ask, was I a fool? Probably so, but I was happy that I had someone to love me. Yes, I believed that he loved me. Even though he'd done a lot of things to almost break my heart into a million pieces he was damn good at patching things up. He bought me everything I could think of following that night. He'd even come home before the sun came up. Getting him in before four AM was definitely unusual but I was getting used to it. He'd also managed to keep Ms. Nyssa out of our lives. He brought his son around and I began to enjoy playing the stepmom role. We were becoming a family made for TV and I felt that things could only go up from that point.

I didn't want to upset him so I quickly maneuvered through traffic. The last thing I needed was an argument.. As hard as I tried I still made it home about fifteen minutes late. I knew that he'd be pissed but hell, I had to fight through traffic to get there.

"Damn, Diamond, what took you so long? I said five o'clock," he yelled, as he walked toward me.

"I tried, traffic was crazy."

"Where were you at anyway?"

"I stopped by to see my mom."

"Your mom? How the hell did you find her?"

"She was at my grandmom's."

"I'm surprised she wasn't at a crack house!" he laughed. I really didn't find anything funny.

"What is it that you need me to do?" I asked, changing the subject.

"I have this car I need you to drive to south Jersey for me."

"What?"

"Yeah, I need you to take this car over to Jersey.

I'm going to give you the directions. Someone is going to take the car, give you another car, and you drive it back home."

"That doesn't make any sense, Davey. What the hell is in the car?"

"Nothing, I just need you to drop off the car. Simple as that."

"How come you can't do it?"

"Because I'm on probation. You know I can't drive out of state!"

"So there isn't anyone else that can do it for you?"

"What's the problem, Diamond? It's not rocket science. As much shit as I do for you, I just need you to do this one favor. Besides, everyone else is working, that's why I asked you."

"I hope this shit isn't illegal, Davey, you promised that I wouldn't have to be involved in any bullshit."

"Look, are you going to do it or not? I can find another bitch to take your place if you want!"

"Why do you always have to say that, Davey? I know you can find somebody else; I don't need you to keep threatening me with that shit. Just give me the damn directions and the car keys so I can go." I turned so that I wouldn't have to see his face. I hated when he did that and he knew that I would do anything to keep him around. He came up behind me to give me a hug. I still stood there, annoyed by his last comment. He put the keys in my hand as I loosened up a little bit. I didn't want to go but I felt like I had to. He gave me the directions before I headed out to the car, a black Toyota Camry. I still didn't know all of the details of this transaction, but deep down I knew that it was better that way.

I got in and began my drive to south Jersey. There wasn't much traffic as I took the Benjamin Franklin Bridge. I was pretty happy about it because I knew that I would get back pretty fast. I had Lloyd playing on the radio and I bobbed my head and sang along like it was karaoke. It had to be a funny sight seeing me act as if I had a microphone and everything. I was feeling the music but at the same time trying to block out the fact that I was being a mule for Davey. I was so into the music that time went by extremely fast. I was almost to the exit before I knew it and glad that I was almost done and on my way home.

After getting off the exit and taking the small streets to the address that he provided, I parked and hurried out of the car. The neighborhood was pretty quiet. There weren't many people outside except what looked like a few hustlers and some children running around in the street. I knocked on the door and waited for someone to open it. I had to knock a few more times before anyone came.

"Can I help you?" a tall, thin-framed woman asked as she opened the door and looked me up and down.

"Is Benny here?"

"Who the hell are you?" she responded. I figured that this was his woman by the attitude she gave when I asked about him.

"I'm here to drop off a car. Tell him Davey sent me."

"He don't know nobody named Davey."

"What do you mean? Davey sent me here from Philly to drop off a car." I was getting annoyed. I didn't know what the hell type of game they were playing, but I wanted to get this over with so I could leave.

"I just said he don't know nobody named Davey."

"Look, here is the note he gave me with the directions and this address. I'm pretty sure that I came to the right place."

"I don't give a fuck about what you have on that paper. You might as well turn back around and head home 'cause Benny don't know him," she yelled, as she began to close the door shut.

I put my hand on the door to stop her from closing it in my face. "Excuse me, don't shut the door in my face. All you have to do is tell Benny I'm here."

"Unless you want to end up a chalk outline on the ground you better back the fuck up off of my door and take your little prissy ass home!"

I could feel the heat rising in my body. I wanted to push the door open and slap her. I decided against it and turned around to walk back to the car and call Davey. He had a lot of explaining to do. I wasted a big part of my day driving here and to be talked to the way I just had been was definitely not in the plans.

I followed the path back to the car. As I was walking, I noticed how the neighborhood was even quieter than it was when I came. I had a strange feeling but I couldn't put my hands on it. I used the keypad to open the car doors and as soon I attempted to open the door cops swarmed around me. I didn't know what the hell was going on.

"Put your hands on the hood of the car," one officer yelled.

"What did I do?" I asked, as I began to cry. I knew I should have listened to my heart and stayed home.

"You have the right to remain silent, anything you say can and will be held against you in a court of law. . . ."

I couldn't even hear him anymore. I was so detached from the situation you could have pinched me and I wouldn't have budged. *Is he reading me my rights? Am I going to jail?* I didn't understand what happened. After I was frisked they put me in handcuffs and put me in the back of a police car. They proceeded to search the car; I noticed them pointing to something in the trunk. *What the hell was it?* I thought.

I didn't find out what it was until I was being questioned in an interrogation room. There was a small amount of cocaine in the trunk. I went numb. Now I realized why the female was acting like she didn't know what I was talking about. It was a setup, and I couldn't believe Davey put me in the middle of it.

Worst of all, it didn't matter how many times I told them the drugs didn't belong to me, they still treated me like a criminal. I told them over and over again that I didn't know who the drugs belonged to. I was simply supposed to drop off a car. The cops didn't believe me. They had even gone so far as laughing as if I told a joke. I knew there wasn't anything I could say to get me out it so I decided to keep quite and pray for a miracle.

I was placed in a holding cell and after being arraigned the following day I was carted off to a detention center in Philadelphia. I knew at that point it was the end of me and Davey. There was no way I could go back to him after this. He promised that I would never be in the line of fire and that's exactly where I ended up. This was definitely going to ruin my life. It was now that I realized this life isn't so glamorous after all. I couldn't be with a man that didn't care about me the way I cared about him. Davey didn't care and I should have realized that after the cheating and the STD. Me, being a fool in love, I couldn't stop going back. At one point I felt like I needed him. I didn't know any other way to have the best of things without being with him. After this, I would have plenty of time to get my mind right and figure out what I would do once I got out of there. Whatever I decided, running his game was out of the question.

Chapter Ten

Mica: The Glamorous Life

Things with Tyson couldn't have been better. I was enjoying the life that he had blessed me with and I surely wasn't trying to give it up anytime soon. For the most part, we hadn't had many arguments lately. Hell, even his crazy-ass ex Deanna hadn't been calling. I could admit that even though things were rocky between us at times we always managed to put the bad times behind us and move on. I hated arguing. Growing up, yelling was all I heard at home, so I wasn't trying to subject myself to anything that even closely resembled what I grew up around.

With all that had been going on, I still hadn't been able to visit my brother, which bothered me more and more each day. I'd sent letters and made numerous attempts to visit and had still been turned away. What the hell had I done that was so bad? My mom tried to get him to talk to me but I assumed he wasn't too interested since he had yet to reach out to me. I believed that he might have been a little jealous of Tyson. I hadn't been one that the men would fight over growing up, so maybe it was just the fact that he was always used to getting all of my attention. Unfortunately, I was a woman now and he would just have to get over it. I just hoped that he would see that no one could replace him in my life and regardless of any relationship that I pursued he'd always be my big brother and I'd always love him the same. The sad part about it all was that I wasn't able to tell him about it since I was getting the silent treatment.

Tyson had set up a special date for us and I was excited because we didn't usually get to go out much. He was always so busy so I appreciated all of the time that he gave me. I had taken all day to make sure that I had the right outfit, hairstyle, and perfume. I hoped that I wasn't overdressed. He said that our destination was a surprise so I didn't have a clue where we were going. I enjoyed surprises, so honestly it didn't even matter. What mattered was that I was going to be able to spend some much needed alone time with him. I was dressed and ready at nine PM like he wanted me to be. I wished that his ass knew the meaning of punctual because I sat there for another hour and I still hadn't heard from him.

I dialed his cell phone so many times that I lost count. He probably hadn't answered it because he knew that I was going to flip out. I was sure going to have an earful for him. If there was one thing that I hated it was wasting time. I always felt like I could be doing something else and sitting in the house in a little black dress and four-inch stilettos was definitely a great example of that. I mean, unless it was a costume for a sexual fantasy there wasn't any reason to be shitty sharp with nowhere to go.

I was getting sleepy the longer I sat there and angrier by the second. Around 10:45 he came strolling in, drunk as hell. I could smell the liquor from the door. My face was twisted in a knot. I couldn't even stand to look at him I was so furious and to make matters even worse he was carrying an opened Heineken beer in his hand. His clothes were even falling off of him. I stood up from the sofa and gave him an evil stare. If this were TV this would be the part where the steam would begin to shoot from my ears.

"What the hell you all dressed up for?" he asked, still unsteady on his feet.

"What the fuck do you mean, what am I dressed up for? We were supposed to have a special date tonight," I yelled, walking closer to him with my finger pointed. I couldn't believe that he'd forgotten and then had the audacity to come in here pissy drunk.

"What date? Who said we were going on a date?"

"So now you don't remember? I can't believe you, Tyson, every time I think that things are going good for us you go and fuck it up!"

"Fuck it up? You want to talk about who's fucking up, huh? Maybe if you'd stop fussing all the time and fuck me like you're supposed to things would be better."

"Are you kidding me, Tyson? Where the hell did

that come from? You weren't saying that shit last night when you were fucking me and sucking me!"

"Of course not, what nigga is going to say something to fuck up some pussy!"

"Pussy? So is that what I am?"

"That's not what I said. Look, I've been drinking and this shit is blowing my high!"

"Fuck you, Tyson. When your ass is sober remember the shit you just said to me because I sure as hell will," I yelled before grabbing my bag and going to the door. I couldn't believe the shit that just happened. Earlier in the day he called and told me he had something special planned and now he was drunk and had forgotten all about it and me for that matter. To make matters even worse he belittled me. I couldn't even wrap my mind around the things that he said to me. I was hurting and I didn't even care about the fact that it was now pouring outside and I didn't even have a damn umbrella over my head. I just wanted to get away from there, far enough away that he couldn't see or hear me cry.

The only place that I could think of going was my mom's. I hated for her to see me upset since instead of being there to console me she'd probably try and figure out a way for me to get back in good with Tyson. I'm not saying that my mom was selfish or that she didn't care about my being hurt or upset, but she did care about her bills being paid and since they wouldn't be without him, I'm positive she wouldn't be too happy about us fighting. I almost hated to tell her when we were at odds because her reaction was never one that you'd expect from a mother.

I was soaking wet when I got in the car. I sat

there for a few seconds to see if he'd come running out of the house after me. Instead, I was still sitting there for ten minutes looking like a fool. He still hadn't come out and no matter how silly it may sound I was still hoping that he would. I was ready to go back in but that would have made me appear weak. I wasn't weak, but I did love my man. I just hated when he got drunk and no matter how many times I'd been in this same situation I hadn't learned that he wouldn't change.

I'd bet money that most women have been in my shoes whether a little bigger or a little smaller, but we've all loved a man a little more than we should have. I had been a victim of love but I didn't want to give it up. I wanted him to love me just as much as I loved him. Was it possible? I don't know, but what I did know was that he cared about me even if it wasn't as much as I cared for him.

I slowly pulled out of the parking spot and began to drive to my mom's house. I was about five minutes into the drive when my cell phone began to ring. I fumbled through my purse while trying to drive at the same time and managed to get it before it stopped.

"Hello?" I said, without even looking at the caller ID.

"Babe, where are you?"

"*Babe?* So now I'm your babe again?"

"Look, I said I was drunk, now come back home, it's late," he slurred.

"I'm not coming home to be talked to that way again."

"I apologize, okay, just come home so we can go to bed."

"I'll see you tomorrow Tyson, go to bed and get sober."

Click.

I hung up, which was one of the hardest things I'd done since I met him. I wanted to go home but I knew that it wouldn't make me feel any better after the argument we'd had. I looked down at the phone and watched him call over and over again. I turned off the phone to avoid the temptation of answering it and being talked into coming home. I continued the drive over to my mom's house and got soaked again trying to run down the block to her door. I used my key to open up the door. The lights were off and the house was quiet. Good, I thought, since I could sneak up to my old room and go to sleep without her even knowing that I was here. I knew that I couldn't avoid talking to her about what happened but at least I could put it off until the morning.

I walked up the steps and almost into the room when I heard her bedroom door opening. Damn, I thought I was going to make it in.

"What are you doing here?" she asked, standing in her robe, wiping her eyes.

"I need to stay here tonight, Mom. I'll leave in the morning."

"Where's Tyson?"

"He's home, Mom, I just need some rest. Can we talk about this in the morning?"

"No, we can talk about it now. What the hell happened?"

"He came in drunk and said some hurtful things, okay? Things that I don't want to repeat."

"Why not?"

"Why the third degree? All I want to do is lay down, rest my brain, and forget about it. Why do I have to go back and forth with you on this?"

"Because it's after eleven at night and you're in here soaking wet in a little-ass dress like you just left the club. That's why," she yelled. She always made things harder than they actually had to be. I didn't understand why I just couldn't come in there and not be questioned. I mean, damn, can I want to visit? I guess not, since she was interrogating me right now.

"I didn't leave the club, I came from home. Can I at least take off these wet clothes first?"

"Go ahead before your ass catch pneumonia. I don't know why you young girls come out in the worst weather with those little-ass clothes on anyway!" she blurted, before turning around and going back into her room. She left the door open, which told me that she wasn't planning on going to sleep without talking to me. I took my time taking off the dress and putting on a T-shirt. I went into her room, where she was sitting up on the bed waiting.

"So, what happened?"

"It was just an argument. We were supposed to go out but he forgot. I sat in the house dressed and waiting on him until he came in drunk with an attitude. It caused an argument and I decided to leave rather than stay there and keep arguing. He needs to get sober and then we can talk."

"If it's one thing that I learned is that you don't walk away for something so silly. If it was just an argument you could have worked it out. I don't know why the first thing you think to do is run. You're going to lose your man like that."

"No, he's going to lose me like that."

"And then what? What are you going to do without him? You don't have the money or the skills to keep up that lifestyle without him," she yelled.

She was only doing what I expected her to do. One thing about my mother was that she was always the same. You pretty much always knew what she was going to say before she said it. I wished that I had somewhere else to go but I didn't. She was right, I didn't have anything without him but shit, neither did she. I remembered the struggle and how I had to work to help her pay the damn bills in here. I didn't want to admit it but I had to go home. I wasn't trying to go back to where I'd been before him.

This life was something that I had become accustomed to. I wasn't going home tonight but tomorrow I would find him and try to get things back in place. I'd be damned if another woman was going to come and take my place. The glamorous life had its downside: you had to fight to keep your place. I had to stop sweating the small stuff and learn how to turn things back around.

Chapter Eleven

Diamond: A Place Called Home

Prison, a place that I'd never thought I would be forced to live. How can a person get comfortable being here? From the moment I walked through the door and had to strip down ass naked to wash and be searched, I knew glamour was no longer a part of my vocabulary. The jumpsuits were huge and smelled like they'd been washed in the cheapest detergent you could use. I was itching from head to toe just thinking about the fact that someone else had worn it before me and I didn't care how many times it had been washed, I still felt my skin crawl.

The first week was the hardest for me. I cried silently every night, wondering how I could have been so foolish. It took everything in me not to tie knots in the sheets and hang myself. Here I was the pretty girl that once had it all donning an orange jumpsuit and sneakers without shoelaces.

It was embarrassing and I could just see all the bitches in the hood laughing and chanting. Miss Diamond the diva had gotten what was coming to her after all. Was that really the case? Was this what I deserved? I couldn't allow myself to believe that, since I'd probably be worse off if I did.

My cell mate, a woman named Tiny, was eventually my savior. At one of my lowest points she was there to help me get the pep back in my step. I didn't believe that I would ever meet a person who was as foolish as me when it came to men, but she was also locked away because she'd do anything for her man.

It had been a long day and I was exhausted. You never really realize how stress can make you even more tired than you actually are. I lay in bed staring at the ceiling thinking about the time I had left there. Soon tears began to flow, and as quiet as I tried to be I guess that it wasn't quite enough because Tiny heard me even in her sleep.

"Crying isn't going to make your time shorter in here," she said as she sat on the side of her bed.

"Excuse me?" I asked, offended by the comment. Of course I knew that crying wouldn't make my time any shorter, but being there didn't stop me from having feelings either. Shit, I still had feelings.

"I said, crying won't make your time shorter. Nobody cares about your pain in here. All they care about is making you suffer for the crime that you committed."

"Obviously, I realize that or I wouldn't be here," I snapped. I was annoyed. I never asked her for her damn advice.

"Listen, little mama, there's no need to get all

antsy with me. I'm trying to help you out. Sitting in here depressed is only going to make it worse. You gotta suck it up and deal with it. Shit, this is going to be your home for a while so you may as well make the best of it."

"Make the best of it?" Was she serious? I didn't believe that it was even possible to make the best of a situation like this. I wanted to go home and I'd be damned if I'd get comfortable here.

"Yes, make the best of it. I was just like you when I came in here. I thought that it was the end of the world. Then I realized that I was too young to just give up. Yeah, I made some foolish choices, but I'm smarter than that. I just got caught up with some nigga."

"A nigga, huh. Sounds a lot like me," I replied, surprised that she was even being so honest. She didn't know me from a can of paint. As much as I didn't want to I was getting more relaxed talking to her.

"Shit, that's half of the women in this damn place. None of us saw it coming," she said, lying back down in her bed. "So sleep on it and trust me, in the morning you'll wake up with a new attitude. Do your time, get out, and don't make the same mistake again."

I didn't respond. Instead, I lay there quietly taking it all in. She was right, I couldn't give up. That would prove that he'd won and gotten the best of me after all. There was a time when I would do anything that he wanted me to do. I knew now that I had to be all about me and as selfish as that may sound, there damn sure wasn't anyone else that was going to do it for me.

I woke up the next morning with a new confidence and not even the sloppy-ass food trays we were served could break me down. Before long Tiny and me were the best of friends and I learned a lot from her each day. I think that I clung to her because she'd been there. Though she voluntarily transported drugs for her man, she still could relate to what I'd been through. Her man of five years hadn't stepped up when she got caught, and now she'd have to serve a one-year sentence, leaving her daughter with the man that snitched on her. When I thought that I had it bad, the fact that she had a child made my situation not look as grim. I always wondered how she could be as calm with a child out there to worry about but she was a firm believer in things happening for a reason, and if she wasn't supposed to be here she wouldn't be.

I felt sorry for her and I knew that once I left I would miss our talks. I did promise that we'd keep in touch. I needed a friend like her, someone that would have my back. How did I know this? What's prison without someone trying to test you? I found this out firsthand. After leaving the area where we'd sit and eat we were headed over to the library area. Tiny had been researching her case since the day that she'd been locked away and since I didn't have anything else to do, I helped her out.

Walking down the hall, I didn't notice the stares, but Tiny must have. Soon, I felt something under my feet and I hit the floor. I didn't get a chance to react because Tiny was already all over the girl that had tripped me. The guards came and separated them before hauling them both off to solitary confinement. I later found out that the girl who'd tripped me had been eyeing me since day one. I thought that it had to have been mistaken identity or something because I had never seen her prior to being locked up. Through the grapevine I heard that she and Tiny were once really close and she was pissed that I'd come and taken her place. It was never my intention. I never had any intentions coming in here, not even to survive it.

Either way, this run-in would land Tiny in the hole for two weeks. When they let her out, she looked tired. Tiny was beautiful for a woman with so much fight in her. She stood about five feet eight and appeared to be about a size eight in clothing. She had long hair, which she kept pulled back in a ponytail, showing her round face. Even stripped of glamour you could tell that she was a looker. She hugged me when she entered the cell. I was glad to see her. It was a lonely two weeks.

"Girl, I'm glad to see you. What the hell was that all about, anyway?"

"Doesn't matter, girl, it's over now."

"Well, thanks for having my back."

"No problem, I know you'd do the same for me."

Would I? I guess it was at that moment when I realized that I would. Anyone that would stick their neck out for me would definitely get the same from me. I realized that she would be here long after I'd left but she'd definitely be my friend either way. It took this situation to know where home really was and I was comfortable laying my head down each night knowing she was by my side.

Chapter Twelve

Mica: The Battle Within

"Come on, Deidra, stay with me. I can't lose you now." Tears were pouring out of my eyes as the ambulance driver sped through traffic with his siren on. The paramedic continued to administer CPR but she still wasn't responding. I couldn't lose her. I didn't have a lot of family and she and I had grown close in the past months.

What the hell had happened? I didn't understand how things had gone so wrong. We had planned to hit the town for the night to celebrate D's birthday. She'd promised me that she wouldn't get high that night and instead have a drug-free good time. All I remember is her opening the door and barely standing up straight. She walked away from the door after letting me in and soon fell to the floor. I ran over to her and once I noticed that she was foaming at the mouth I grabbed the phone and dialed 911.

I prayed that this wouldn't be the end. To die on your birthday, how ironic is that? She had been through so much growing up and even as an adult; to just simply die this way didn't seem right. I was losing it, sitting here on this bench clinging to her hand. It was stiff but warm, which gave me hope that she was still holding on.

Though it only took about ten minutes to reach the hospital, it seemed like forever. It was as if everything was moving in slow motion and I was on the outside looking in. She was rushed to the trauma room and I was told to wait in the waiting room. I paced back and forth. I couldn't even think. I hadn't even called Tyson to let him know what was going on. What was I going to say? He didn't like me around her anyway, since he assumed that her bad habits would rub off on me.

I would go up to the window every ten minutes or so to ask about her and each time I was pointed back in the direction of the waiting area. The woman at the counter was obviously annoyed since after a while she stopped speaking and just pointed her fingers instead. I didn't give a fuck about her attitude. That was my cousin dying in there. She was lucky to have the thick bulletproof glass in front of her because I was ready to break that damn finger off. The longer I waited I felt that the prognosis wouldn't be good. Damn, had I just come earlier that day I probably could have swayed her away from using in the first place.

After I'd waited for about an hour, someone finally came out and escorted me to the back of the ER. I was nervous as I followed the female doctor in all green scrubs. She was pretty quiet and wouldn't say a word as we walked what seemed like a mile. She took me into a small conference room and shut the door.

"Have a seat," she said, pointing to the green cushioned chairs that matched the ones that I'd been sitting in for the past hour. Once this day was over, I never wanted to see a green chair again in my life. "Deidra is doing much better than when she was brought in so you can relax."

I let out a sigh of relief. I thought for sure I would hear the worse. "So what happened?"

"She had a seizure, which was caused by a drug withdrawal. A drug addict's system gets used to the drug and eventually depends on it like our body depends on food and water. When they try to go cold turkey without any help it sometimes has bad effects. The extreme could be what you witnessed today or even worse, death. Luckily, she made it here on time or else she might not have made it."

Was I really hearing her right? Withdrawal? So, D was actually trying to quit? What the hell would make her do that? I knew that my talks with her made a lot of sense to me, but, damn, I hadn't gotten through any other time so there had to be something other than that to make her change so drastically. Either way, I was glad that she made it out okay.

"So what does that mean?"

"She should probably be checked into an inpatient rehab. It's great that she wants to quit but she has to do it the right way. I can give you a list of treatment centers and you could go over them with her and maybe she'll make the right decision."

"When can I see her?"

"You can actually see her right now, she's awake but a little groggy. I'll take you in the back where you can see her."

She led me out to the room where they'd taken D. She smiled when she saw me, I smiled as well. I had never been happier to see her.

"Baby girl, I scared the hell out of you, huh?"

"Scared isn't the word. What the hell were you thinking?"

"I was trying to quit. I know that I'm pretty much all that you have out here in this world, and prior to you showing up on my door that day, I didn't give a damn about life. Now, I care. I care about you a lot. More than you may believe." She grabbed hold of my hand as I sat on the edge of the bed.

I never dreamed that someone would care about me that much. I know some people would think it was bull for a lifelong drug addict to want to change because they love someone, but honestly, I believe it was a combination of loving and being loved at the same time. Her family shut her out and when I came around and showed her how much I cared it helped her see things in a totally different light.

We sat and talked for what seemed like hours. I didn't want to leave but eventually I had to. Once I left I headed home. I was ready for a blowout with Tyson since it was now three AM and I hadn't called him to let him know where I was. As soon as I walked in the living room he began ranting. I damn sure was in no mood for his temper tantrums.

"Where the hell were you?"

"Tyson, please don't start. I've had a very long night and I don't feel like arguing with you."

"Who's arguing? I just asked a damn question. It'll only turn into an argument if you don't answer me."

"Listen, D got sick and I had to call an ambulance to take her to the hospital."

"She got sick? A drug addict? They can handle anything, you expect me to believe that?"

"Yes, I do, because it's the truth. She damn near died, Tyson. If I would have showed up just a few minutes later she might have been gone for good."

"You're real smart, Mica. You deserve a damn Oscar. I'm going out, call me when you're ready to tell me the truth about where you really were all fucking night!"

I didn't respond. I knew that he wouldn't believe me. Most men that are out doing dirt believe that you are doing the same shit, so they never think you're telling the truth. I wasn't out doing dirt—shit, I hadn't did anything wrong since dating him. I cared about him too much to cheat but that shit didn't matter. He was stuck in his own world and it didn't matter what I told him, he still would assume that I was lying. I headed up to bed and after saying a prayer climbed in and got comfortable.

I visited Deidra the next day and told her how foolish Tyson had acted when I came home. She assured me that things would get better. He was probably guilty about something and it would either come to light or pass by. I didn't spend too much time on that topic since I wanted to forget it and focus on her recovery. She decided to go to an inpatient rehab for three weeks and continue the treatment as an outpatient after that. I was happy with that and I felt like things could only go up from that point. She had a three-day hospital stay and checked into the rehab with confidence. It would take a lot of determination to win the battle within, but I planned on helping her every step of the way.

Chapter Thirteen

Diamond: Free to Roam

After my nine-month stay in the Philadelphia Federal Detention Center, I knew that I had to change my life for the better. Looking back, I couldn't figure out how I ended up where I was. I had no family to run to, I had no man or money. I definitely had to get my strategy together to figure out how I was going to get back to the top. I had no access to money and luckily I could stay at Kiki's until I got back on my feet. I had a degree in accounting but had never actually worked anywhere. Davey had always supplied me with more than enough money, so I felt that a job wasn't necessary. I wished that I had used my brain because now I was in a position that I had never been very fond of. It reminded me of the hard times living at my grandmom's. There were plenty of times that our only source of nourishment was from Oodles of Noodles and Hug juices. Now, you couldn't pay me to eat any of that shit. I'd rather starve than eat anything less than what I felt I deserved. I know that may sound conceited and in my current position some would probably say I should eat whatever the hell I could get my hands on, but that wasn't me.

Kiki loaned me a few dollars to get my hair and nails done. If I was going to go out looking for a new man I had to at least look the part. I headed to the salon that I used to go to on a regular basis before I got locked up and found out just how much things had changed in such a short time. When I walked in everyone instantly got quiet except Gea, my hairdresser, who damn near knocked me down running over to give me a hug.

"Girl, I am so happy to see you. You look good, girl!" she said, looking me up and down.

"What was I supposed to look like?" I said, playfully putting one hand on my hip. I guess people thought that I would come out looking a wreck. I guess I proved them wrong when I walked up in there still clad in designer gear from head to toe. Kiki had managed to gather some of my things from Davey's house when I got locked up and held onto them for me. "I'm glad to be here, girl. I can't wait to get back on my job!" I said, laughing. My job meaning scooping me up a nigga with cash.

All of the girls in the neighborhood had dreams of catching dudes with money like Davey. The problem with most of them was that they appeared too desperate for the money. Niggas weren't going to just give their cash away so if it was too obvious that your main goal was to tap their bank, you would get played in the end. I had mastered the trick of getting their attention and keeping it, but this time around I had to make sure that I didn't fall victim and end up like I had done the last time.

Soon, I was in Gea's chair getting my hair pressed and curled. By then, the crowd in the shop had loosened up and I was getting caught up on all of the gossip.

"Girl, you know Kemp Lo is a free agent now," one girl, said turning her lip up on one side.

"What? He finally let Deja go? I can't believe that. You know the bitches are going to be flocking to him like pigeons all that damn money he got!" another female said, slapping the other one high five and laughing.

My ears instantly became glued to the conversation. Kemp Lo? That was a name that I had never heard, but I was sure interested in hearing it again. I loved a nigga with money and the way they talked about him he seemed like he was just my type. I wanted to ask more about him but I knew that it would seem too obvious if I did. I decided to wait and do some research. I had to know who he was, especially since he was single, which was every reason for me to place myself in his view.

After I left the salon and headed back to Kiki's, I couldn't ask her fast enough if she knew who Kemp was.

"Kemp Lo, yeah, I know him. Why?" she asked, washing dishes and glancing at the television.

"I heard them talking about him in the salon today and I wanted to know who he was."

"Girl, when are you going to learn, these hustlers don't mean you no good. Wasn't nine months in jail bad enough?"

"What the hell else am I going to do? I have a record now, so getting a good job is out of the question. I need to get back on top, Kiki, and that's the only way that I know how," I replied. That was the only way I knew how to be on top. I knew how to be on the bottom too, and I wasn't trying to stay there for too much longer.

She looked at me for a few seconds before speaking, probably wondering how a girl as smart as me could be so stupid. She turned off the faucet and took a seat at the kitchen table and lit a cigarette. Taking a puff of her Newport, she began revealing the information that I was desperate to hear.

"Kemp Lo is a major hustler, I mean *major*. Not a lot of females even get him to look their way. He used to deal with a girl named Deja, last I heard. They have a child together too that he spoils to death. It's a rumor that Kemp has millions in a safe buried somewhere. People only speculate where it is but no one's ever found it. He's fine as hell for sure and he commands everyone's attention when he walks into a room. Now, I've also heard that he's abusive, so I wouldn't run to jump in his bed if I were you. I mean, you've been through enough ups and downs with that other asshole. I know that I can't stop you from dealing with him if that's what you want to do, but don't ever say I didn't warn you. You are my girl and I want to see you happy. I never want to see you in a situation like the one you just got out of."

"I know, Kiki, and believe me, I don't want to be

in another fucked-up relationship either. I was real naive with Davey, but this time I'm on my game. This isn't about finding love, it's about finding money. I need to get me enough money so I can make it on my own. It's just a stepping stone, Kiki. I promise you I won't end up like I did the last time," I said, grabbing hold of her hand. I appreciated her warnings, and trust me, I took heed to them. I knew what I needed to do, and I was so focused on it. I didn't plan on falling in love. For me, that wasn't an option.

"I believe you, girl, but I need you to be careful, okay? Don't get yourself hurt."

"I won't, girl. I promise."

I needed to find him just to see what all the fuss was about. I planned on following him around until I figured out a way to get close to him. I was beautiful, but there were a lot of beautiful women out there, so the key was to get his attention and make him believe that I was the one he needed to be with. I didn't think it was going to be too hard, but I was soon going to find out.

I followed him for weeks. It didn't matter where he went, I made sure I was watching from a distance. Some would probably think that I was crazy, but I had to do my research before I stepped into any situation. I wasn't about to go into it blind like I had done before. I wasn't going to get fooled. Kiki thought I was nuts for what I was doing, but since she was usually the voice of reason, what she said went in one ear and out the other. I wasn't in the state of mind for reasoning since I had my eye on the prize. I just had to keep my eyes wide open and not fall in love like I'd done in the past.

I had done it without being noticed until one day I headed into the barbershop where he got his hair cut. I was bold this particular day because I wanted him to see. I was sure that he'd seen me around on other occasions, but I wanted him to at least get a close-up. I found a local promoter who had an event coming up and needed some help with promotion. I was eager to help since passing out his flyers and posters would make it less obvious that I was everywhere that Kemp was. Dressing up and hitting the streets was a guaranteed way to get in a hustler's view. Most girls used this method, but the difference between them and me was that I was going to get more than a fuck. Most guys felt like the women who tried too hard to get their attention were only good for sex anyway. Philly was party central, and if you wanted to meet a baller you had to get out into the nightlife. It just took a little skill to snag the right one without seeming too obvious. Me, I wouldn't make it obvious, and once I got his attention it would be all over.

I put on the shortest pair of shorts that I owned and a tight tank top with some heels. Yes, heels. I wasn't really going to be walking around in them all day but just long enough to catch his eye. I walked in to Big D's barbershop with a stack of flyers and a few posters in my hand. As soon as I walked in of course every eye was on me, including Kemp's. I went over to D's chair and asked if it was okay for me to leave the flyers and put a couple of posters in the window. Once he agreed I put on my model strut to place the flyers on the counter. I even walked up to every man in there and put one in their hands. I stood in front of Kemp just a few seconds longer so he could get a whiff of the perfume that I was wearing. He slowly lifted his hand to take the flyer from me.

"Are you going to be here at this party? If so, I'll make sure I'm there!" He laughed, looking down at the flyer.

"Most likely I will be."

He smiled. "Good, hope to see you there."

"Count on it," I said, returning a smile and heading toward the door.

Damn, I thought for sure that he would have tried to put a move on me, but I guess since he was in front of all these guys he had to keep it basic. I didn't care; I knew I would get him eventually. It was just going to take a little longer than I thought.

The week went fast and it was party time. I felt so good going out. The nine months that I spent locked away felt like an eternity. Now that I was free to roam I was going to party like there was no tomorrow. I had to enjoy myself. Shit, I deserved it after all I'd been through.

The party was at a club called ICE, and Kiki was able to hang out with me. I was excited about going with the hopes that I would run into Kemp there. The party was packed and the line outside was damn near curving around the corner. Luckily, we knew the bouncer and were able to skip it. I might have contemplated leaving if I'd had to wait in that long-ass line. We squeezed through the crowd and made our way to the bar. It was like pulling teeth to get the bartenders' attention. Niggas were so rude, damn near pushing us out of the way to get their drinks. I was getting annoyed, and if I didn't get a drink soon to mellow me out I would probably be on my way back out of the door.

I felt an arm reaching over my shoulder and I was ready to lose it. I turned around and had a shocked look on my face when I saw that it was Kemp. I hoped the look wasn't too obvious, but figured it probably was since he started laughing.

"Damn, did you see a ghost or something?" He continued to laugh.

"No, it's just too crowded in here and I'm getting annoyed because the bartenders are acting like we are invisible," I yelled in his ear over the loud music.

"I feel you, but if y'all want to come over in VIP we're popping bottles over there."

A tall, thin-framed guy came up behind him and tapped him. He turned around and the guy told him something that quickly made him walk away without even turning back around to me. I was pissed. Damn, I hadn't even gotten a chance to tell him my name. I grabbed Kiki and tried to make it over to the VIP area, and when we peeked in we noticed that Kemp and his friends were all gone.

"Damn, where did they go?"

"Girl, I don't know. You said someone came and told him something. Something must have gone wrong if they all just picked up and left."

I pouted and Kiki laughed. I didn't find it funny.

I knew now that I had to get more creative if I wanted to make it happen. Just being in his eye-sight wasn't enough.

"Stop looking like a sad puppy." She continued to laugh.

"I'm upset, girl. I thought that this was going to be my chance."

"You'll get your chance, D. Things happen when they are supposed to."

I knew that what she said was true but I wasn't a true believer in that saying. I always believed that the go-getters were the ones that had it all. You weren't going to get shit if you just sat back all the time and waited for things to happen because "they happen when they are supposed to." I felt like things happened when you took the initiative to make them happen. Either way, I knew that I had gotten his attention, even if only for a few seconds.

Kiki and I stayed at the club until it closed. I was so drunk but I had fun, which was something else that I hadn't done in a long time. We went back to her house and as soon as my head hit the pillow I could feel myself drifting off into la-la land. Tomorrow was going to be a better day and I went to sleep satisfied with that.

Chapter Fourteen

Mica: That Old Thing

"**B**abe, come on, if we don't get down there early enough we won't get a good seat," I yelled loud enough so that Tyson could hear me.

"I'm coming," he yelled, before coming down the steps.

We were headed down to South Street to the Laugh House, a comedy club that had stand-up Thursdays. I loved to get a seat early because I'd be damned if I was going to walk into a comedy show late so they could talk about me. Comedians were good for that. I wasn't trying to be the butt of anyone's jokes. I was excited about hanging out with Tyson. Since our last fight things had gotten back on track and we were closer than ever. He said that he wanted to do something special because it was our one-year anniversary. It seemed like yesterday that I met him and fell in love with him.

We got down to the show just before it started and made it in without incident. I felt relieved. The comedians kept me laughing all night. I was practically rolling on the floor at their jokes. I needed to laugh—they say laughter is good for the soul.

I remembered growing up and not having a lot to laugh about. Since my dad was always drunk, cussing and fussing all the time we never really got the chance to be a close family. I wanted to be like the families you seen on TV. Hell, I didn't even know if families like that actually existed. I vowed that whenever I had children I'd be sure not to subject them to anything that could damage the people they would later become.

I can admit that I was damaged. It wasn't something I was proud of, but I knew it was the reason that I wasn't confident enough to do things on my own. I felt like I needed a man, and I didn't really know why. It could have been the fact that my mother went crazy after my father was gone. Was it the loss of my father that sent her into depression or was it simply the fact that she didn't have a man to take care of her anymore? I never wanted people to think that I couldn't do for myself, but it was reality.

Since things were going good between Tyson and me I wasn't going to jinx it and think that something bad was going to happen. I wanted to look at the future and be confident that things could only go up from here.

The show was over around ten o'clock and we went back home. Tyson told me to wait five minutes before coming in the house. I laughed because he was actually trying to be romantic. Romance wasn't his department, but if he could pull this off it would impress me.

"Five minutes, I'm not trying to stay out here alone," I said, trying to hurry it up.

"Babe, I'm trying to do something special here. You always say that I'm not romantic. Five minutes won't kill you." He smiled.

His smile warmed my heart, so much so that I agreed. I wasn't really trying to stay outside alone, but he was right, five minutes to get to ecstasy wasn't going to kill me. I watched him walk inside and instantly began watching the seconds on my watch like a hawk. Five short minutes seemed like an eternity but once the time was up I ran up to the door like it was the half-off sale at David's Bridal.

As I walked up to the door I could hear the music playing along with the flickering of candlelight shining through the window. As I slowly opened the door, the lavender aroma tickled my nose, immediately sending chills up and down my spine. I took off my shoes at the door so I could feel the plush carpet underneath my tired feet. A pink piece of paper caught my attention and I made my way over to the table to retrieve it. The note simply read: *Take off your clothes*. I didn't waste any time obeying and after I was naked I wondered what to do next. I didn't see any more notes posted so I slowly wandered through the house trying to find the next clue. Once I noticed the trail of rose petals leading to the bathroom I knew exactly where to go.

The lights were dim and as I entered the room there was another note sitting on the table next to the sink that read: *Get in*. I smiled as I set the note back down next to the plate of chocolate-covered strawberries and two champagne flutes filled to the brim on a sliver serving tray. I thought, *Damn, he's really trying to show off.* He hadn't done anything this nice since we'd been together. I was enjoying it tremendously and I hadn't even seen him yet. I eased into the tub full of hot water that soothed my body. I hoped that I wouldn't fall asleep and ruin his plans since the water felt so good against my skin. I sat in the water and before closing my eyes Tyson appeared with a towel around his waist.

"Baby, this is—" I tried to speak but he quickly bent down to kiss me. His lips were soft as silk and I was eager to feel them on the sensitive parts of my body. He grabbed a sponge and after lathering it up with soap he made slow circles on my back. Though he'd washed my back for me many times, it had never felt so good.

I didn't say a word but instead let him lead. After washing my entire body he grabbed me by the hand and as I stepped out of the tub the excess water trickled down my body. He stood back and licked his lips as he watched the glow my wet figure had. I could sense how bad he wanted to taste me and I couldn't wait until he was able to get his wish. He grabbed a towel from the cabinet and started to dry me off after I stepped out of the tub. My nipples stood at attention as he brushed past them. We walked into the bedroom where the bed was also covered with rose petals. He grabbed a strawberry off of the serving tray that he had carried from the bathroom and after I lay across the bed he kissed my lips with it. The chocolate melted instantly from the heat of my body. He moved close to me and licked the few drops off of my lips.

He began to suck on my erect nipples, causing my body to shiver. His tongue continued to caress them as his fingers found their way to my clit. He made circles on it, quickly causing my already juicy mound to explode. He used his thick tongue to move in and out of my tunnel. He pushed my legs up in the air so that my ass lifted off of the bed just enough to create a wider opening. He ate my pussy for what seemed like an eternity, giving me so much pleasure. After my body shook uncontrollably he knew his mission was complete. He sat up, and as I watched him lick my juices from his lips I prepared myself to satisfy him the same as he'd done me.

He removed the towel that he had around his waist, revealing his hard dick. I couldn't wait to taste it. I motioned for him to lie down on the bed. I looked into his eyes as I moistened the head of his dick. Both of us were in heaven, and I enjoyed the taste of his pre-cum running down my throat. I used my fingertips to massage his balls as I licked his shaft and watched his body begin to tremble. I contracted my cheek muscles and moved up and down his thick member. As the head met my tonsils, I used my deep-throating skills to satisfy him the best way that I knew how. While my throat muscles massaged the head, my hands massaged his balls. Soon I could feel the hot cum shooting down my throat, and I swallowed it with ease. I continued to suck wildly as his knees trembled. I refused to let go, and within minutes his once semi-soft member was hard as a rock and ready to meet my hot, juicy tunnel.

I quickly straddled him, slowly easing him into my tight pussy, and a moan escaped him. I moved back and forth with my hands on his muscular chest. The excitement had me sweating, which got me moving faster. I was riding him like a winning racehorse. My prize would be an electrifying orgasm, and as I felt his dick begin to pulsate I decreased my speed to tap my clit with each stroke. Soon I grabbed ahold of his hands as we exploded together.

We had gotten that old thing back that I missed and I wanted to pause this moment, hoping that things wouldn't ever change.

Chapter Fifteen

Diamond: Fly like Me

*B*oom.

I held my breath, hoping this would go the way that I had planned. I had run Kiki's car into the back of Kemp's brand-new Mercedes-Benz GL-Class truck. I only tapped it enough to cause him to stop. I didn't really want to do any damage. Kemp's door flew open and I saw the anger in his face. I was almost afraid to get out of the car, but sitting there wouldn't get me any closer to him.

"What the fuck, your brakes don't work?" he yelled, walking toward the back of his car to see what damage had been done.

I nervously got out of the car, adjusted my mini-skirt, and began walking toward him. "I am so sorry; I almost dropped a hot cup of coffee on my leg. I tried to stop, I'm really sorry." I batted my eyelashes as I bent down to look at the back of his truck, which only had a tiny scratch on it. I made sure to reveal as much leg as possible while he stood in back of me.

He changed his tone. "It's cool, ma. You only scratched it a little." I knew that I had him right where I wanted him. "What's your name?"

"Diamond," I replied, standing up and focusing all of my attention on him.

"If you were anybody else, I would have snapped. I didn't expect a beautiful woman like you to be behind the wheel. My name is Kemp. It's nice to meet you, Diamond," he spoke, reaching his hand out to shake mine. His hands were smooth as a baby's butt and his nails were perfectly manicured. I smiled, waiting for what he would say next. "You hang out with that girl Kiki, right?"

"Yeah, that's like my big sister."

"I know, I've been seeing you a lot lately. Are you new to the hood?"

"No, I was away for a little while. I just came back."

"Well look, do you have a number I can reach you at? I'd love to finish up this conversation but I have some business to take care of."

"Yeah, I do," I said, grabbing his cell phone out of his hand to put my number in. He looked at me with a grin that could make you melt. I was getting moist just thinking about spending time with him. "I hope to hear from you soon," I said, as I gave the phone back to him.

"Trust me, you will. Keep looking sexy like that and you won't be able to get rid of me." He licked his lips and smiled, heading toward his car.

I turned to walk away and put on a switch as I

did to make sure he would really make that call. Shit, if he didn't I would have to find another way to get his attention. I was determined to be the next woman on his arm and the more I was warned about him the more that I wanted to get next to him. I knew that most people would think I was crazy, especially looking at the situation that I had just gotten out of. I wasn't crazy; I was just a girl with a goal, a goal to be on top and not let anyone take me under.

I headed back to Kiki's to tell her my good news. I knew she wouldn't be all that amused, but hell, I was ecstatic. I was so close to that success that I could taste it. Once I got to her place I found her cleaning up the kitchen while singing to a music video on BET. You couldn't tell her anything when it came to singing. Kiki thought she was Mary J. Blige, Faith Evans, and Beyoncé all wrapped up in one. Quiet as it's kept, she couldn't sing a lick, but I refused to break her spirit.

"Hey girl, I got some good news, bad news, and some more good news to make up for the bad news," I said, turning down the volume on the television so that she could give me her undivided attention.

"This better be good since you're interrupting my jam," she said, laughing.

"Okay, first I ran into Kemp Lo today and I think that I've caught his eye."

"Who says that's good news?" she replied, sarcastically.

"Me, of course, but I ran into the back of his car today and—"

"With my car?" She turned, looking at me in shock without letting me finish up the sentence that I had started.

"Yes, but it only has a few scratches. The other good news is that he has my number and he's going to call me. So once he gets a whiff of this girl, he'll be like putty in my hand and if the money is like everyone claims, I'll be able to buy you a new car!"

"Really, what makes you think that he won't treat you just like everyone else?" she asked, not impressed with my hopes.

"Because I'm Diamond and he's never had a bitch like me," I laughed, as I took a seat on the stool. "He won't be able to do nothing but treat me like a queen once he gets a taste. I stand by that shit, one hundred percent."

"Well, I hope that it works out for you, because I could use a new car." She joined in my laughter, while slapping me a high five.

I knew that she wanted me to be happy and probably deep down hoped that things would go my way. I promised myself that I would never be hurt again so going into this I was at a different place mentally than I had ever been with relationships.

I hadn't heard from Kemp following the accident. Three weeks had passed and I was beginning to get nervous that he might have found someone else. I had to find out where he would be so that I could get in his eye view again. I wasn't trying to be a stalker or anything; I simply called it keeping my eye on the prize.

So, once again I was on the hunt and again it paid off. I found out that he was going to a Sixers game on Wednesday of that week. Of course he had box seats so I had to see how the hell I could get some to even get up to the area where the doors were. Kiki was able to talk to a friend of hers that worked down at the Wachovia Center to get me a pass to go down to the box-seat level. What the hell was I doing? Was I going overboard? No, I snapped back to reality. I wasn't going overboard, I was doing what I had to do and I didn't really care what anybody thought.

Once I gained access to the level of the boxes I had to look for the one that was his. The Wachovia Center was pretty big so I had to damn near walk around the entire circle before I found it.

As I slowly walked past the door that led to his box I prayed that someone would walk out. Unfortunately, no one did. There was a guy standing outside of the door who I assumed was a guard. I headed over to him and took a chance; the worst thing that could happen was that he would turn me away. I could hear the chants from inside the box the closer that I got to the door. I prayed that Kemp didn't have a female with him inside because that would completely crush my plans.

"Excuse me, but is this Kemp's box?" I asked, batting my eyelashes and trying to look as irresistible as possible.

"Yeah, why?" he responded with a dry tone.

"I'm here in a box down the way and I just wanted to say hi to him if that's possible."

"Well, he doesn't like being interrupted while watching the game."

"I'm sure if you tell him that it's me he won't mind," I responded, hoping that what I just said was true. "My name is Diamond, could you just tell him that I'm out here?"

He looked me up and down for a few seconds before responding, "Wait right here." He opened up the door and quickly closed it behind him.

I stood patiently and waited for him to emerge. To my surprise Kemp appeared instead of the guard. I smiled when I saw his face.

"What's up, sexy? How did you know I was here?" he said, reaching out to give me a hug.

I gladly accepted the hug and held onto him as long as I could. "Everybody knows you're here. I just wanted to stop by and say hi. You never did make that phone call that you promised."

"I know, I've been busy as hell but I will. You want to come hang out inside?"

"I wish I could but I'm here with some friends. I just wanted to say hi and see your face again."

"See my face, huh? You sure that's all you wanted to do?"

"Well, that's all I want to do at the moment," I said, putting my head down, trying to avoid eye contact. He was turning me on but I couldn't let it be too obvious.

"You don't have to be shy with me, tell me what you really want," he said, moving so close to me I could feel his breath on my forehead.

"What I really want is to see what you have that drives all the women wild."

"You sure about that?" he asked, as he gently touched my chin to raise my head.

"I'm positive." I looked him in the eye. *What the hell was I getting myself into?* I thought as we stood so close I could feel the heat from his body. Without saying another word he grabbed me by the hand and walked toward the door. He looked back at me before opening it. I still didn't know what he planned to do but I went along with it. The room was full of guys. I was nervous once they all turned to look in our direction. After only a few seconds of staring they all turned their attention on the game. He led me toward the small bathroom in the corner of the room and closed the door behind us. I still was silent. I was wearing a knee-length dress and shirt that generously showed my cleavage. Kemp picked me up and sat me on the sink where he moved close, tilted my head to the side, and began to kiss my neck. How he knew that was my spot, I'll never know but I did know that I instantly became wet when he made contact. My nipples were as hard as a rock peering through my shirt. Just the feeling of him rubbing against them made me tingle all over as I tried not to make enough noise to be heard through the door. His hands made their way down to my underwear than he quickly removed and got back in position, paying close attention to my neck. His thick fingers were now massaging my wet pussy down below.

"Damn, this pussy is wet," he said, as he slid two fingers inside of me. I was about to explode but I didn't want to waste it all over his fingers. I'd rather cum all over his tongue or his dick for that matter. I held onto it as he finger-fucked me and continued licking my neck at the same time. I tried to rub his dick through his jeans but he wouldn't let me. I loved a man to take control. In one motion he dropped his pants and put on a condom. I didn't even know where the hell he got it from, he was so quick. Before I could even think about it his dick was filling my walls from end to end. He grabbed me lightly around my neck and fucked me with force. I loved the rough shit from time to time so this definitely excited me. I grabbed ahold of his ass to force him all the way inside of me, making sure to hit my G-spot. My legs were wrapped around him, not wanting to let go.

"You like this shit?"

"Yes," I moaned. I more than liked it, I fucking loved it. His dick was perfect, the right length, girth, and curve. Who could ask for anything more? I was in heaven as he continued to move in and out of me. I was trying to keep my ass from falling into the sink and keep his dick tightly nestled in my pussy where it belonged.

He continued to fuck me like there was no tomorrow, and I was in a trance, enjoying the strokes that he delivered. My hands were cuffed around his neck. I could feel the muscles flexing as he continued to move in and out of me. It wasn't long before his body was shaking and we were both having orgasms in sync.

"So where do we go from here?" he asked.

I was surprised by that question. I didn't know what to say. I knew what I wanted to happen at this point, but I wasn't sure what he wanted. As I got up off the sink and began to fix my clothes, I looked up at him and replied, "Depends on you. You like to fly coach or first class?"

He looked at me and smiled. "A nigga like me only goes first class."

"Well, in that case, we can work something out 'cause I'm a fly bitch. You ain't gonna find another chick like me."

He laughed. I was dead serious. I was dressed by then and looked in the mirror to make sure my hair was straight. I couldn't go out of the door looking crazy because they'd know for sure what we had been doing in there. He said he would call later on that night. I was smiling from ear to ear as we headed out of the bathroom and toward the door of the box. The guys inside just looked and smiled; they knew what was up. I walked out of there with confidence because I knew that after that sample he just had, he'd definitely call. Who could turn down a girl like me?

That night I did get the phone call that he promised and after that day we spent all of his free time together. I never thought that he would be the type that cared or showed his feelings, but he surprised me everyday. The more I tried not to care about him the more I did. He was hard to resist and I was losing sight of the reason I sought out after him in the first place. I learned a lot about him but the most important thing I learned was how much he was really worth and where he kept his money. I guess he felt comfortable telling me all of this. Why? Because I made him love me. I did everything perfect. He sometimes thought that I was too perfect but I knew better.

I moved in with him about three months after we were together and I was happy to have a permanent place to stay. Things hadn't gone so good for me since getting out of jail, so he was making my life enjoyable. Besides the occasional hood rat calling and yelling obscenities we didn't really have too many problems. Things were good for us and I felt like I was finally where I belonged.

Chapter Sixteen

Mica: Risky Business

I had just gotten four brand-new tires on my car because they were slashed. I was pissed when I walked outside to find them all slashed again. *Who the fuck is doing this?* I knew that it was probably one of Tyson's groupies trying to make a point. I wasn't afraid, but I was pissed and whoever it was better hope that I didn't find them because it was definitely going to be a confrontation.

I had shit to do and this was an inconvenience. I went back into the house to call Tyson and tell him I needed his car for the day. His cell phone kept ringing and going to voice mail. Soon the phone started ringing but it was a blocked number. I started not to answer it but I did just in case it was Tyson calling me back.

"Hello!" I yelled into the receiver

"Guess you can't go anywhere without wheels,

huh?" the female on the other end burst into laughter.

"Who the fuck is this?"

"Ask your man, he just got through licking my pussy too so you may not want to kiss him unless you like eating pussy too!" She continued to laugh.

"Listen bitch, you can keep flattening the tires; it won't make him leave me. You have to come a little harder than that."

"Harder is not a problem, bitch, and don't be so sure about him staying there. He said that you can't fuck anyway!"

"Whatever, you need to grow up whoever the fuck you are. Just know, bitch, you are just another number. He has tons of groupies but I'm the first lady. Have a nice day, bitch!" I said before hanging up.

The phone rang over and over again until I picked it up again, and this time it was Tyson so I was ready to give him an earful.

"Babe, what's going on?"

"What's going on? You have a groupie out here that thinks it's funny to keep flattening my fucking tires."

"What?"

"Yeah, the bitch just called, I just changed the fucking tires last week. If you're gonna cheat, Tyson, keep these bitches in their place!"

"Mica, I don't know who the hell that was."

"I don't know, she didn't say her name and she called from a blocked number. I need you to come home and bring me your car. I have things to do."

"So do I, Mica. I can't come home right now."

"Well, what am I supposed to do? You need to

figure something out, it's your fault that this is happening. If you stop lying to these bitches and tell them you have a girl maybe they wouldn't expect more from you."

"Come on now, don't nobody be lying to these bitches. I can't stop them from doing crazy shit. I don't even know who it is."

"You're fucking that many people that you can't narrow it down to one?"

"You're taking this in a whole different direction."

"Well, how about I help you narrow it down, she said that you just got through licking her pussy so unless you eat pussy for a living now, I'm sure you know who it is. How about you get me a fucking car and take care of that bitch!" *Click.*

I hung up and screamed. I was so pissed. I was even more pissed that he tried to act like he didn't know what the fuck I was talking about. He knew good and goddamn well who he'd fucked. I stood in the living room pacing back and forth. I was close to calling him back but I knew that he probably wouldn't answer the phone anyway. I swear if he had been standing there at that very moment I would've smacked his ass. To me having a relationship should follow the same rules as drug dealing. No female should ever be able to infiltrate the home structure. If it's possible, then the structure is weak. I had gotten used to the fact that he cheated. Shit, all men did. What I wasn't going to stand for was more disrespect. I couldn't stand when a female on the outside had so much control over what we had.

After about an hour he came home. I was sitting on the sofa staring at the TV. He looked at me without speaking and threw his car keys on the table.

"Happy now?"

"Happy? What the hell is wrong with you? I don't understand how you can have an attitude. I didn't do anything to you."

"I don't have an attitude, I just don't feel like arguing. I brought you the keys and the car so you can go do whatever the hell you had to do that is so important. Tim is towing the car and they'll put the tires on today. I'll bring the car back when they're done."

"You do have an attitude," I replied, knowing full well he was upset. "It shouldn't be directed at me; it should be on that bitch that flattened the tires."

"I took care of that already so you don't have to keep fussing about it. You'll get the car back later." He turned to head back out the door.

"That is not what this is about, Tyson. I don't understand why you don't feel like I deserve respect."

"I never said that and I already said I took care of it. This conversation is over, I'm out," he responded before leaving and slamming the door.

How was it that each time we fought he always tried to turn the focus on me like I did something wrong? I was never the one to blame, but he tried his best to make it appear that way. I've never cheated—or even thought about it, for that matter—but he had done it so many times that I lost count. Why is it that when a man gets caught doing wrong they can't just fess up to it and apologize or try to make it better? Instead they either lie or react the way that Tyson had, as if they were the innocent one. I guess it's just in their makeup to lie. The worst part of lying, though, is that most of them weren't smart enough to keep up with the lies so they end up getting caught anyway. Women were smarter in the sense that if when we ever did wrong our tracks were covered. I believed that Tyson's method of covering up his wrongdoings wasn't to lie but merely to make you forget what the hell you were angry about.

I can't say that I blamed him, but I just wished that things with us would run a little smoother. I didn't want to fight, I didn't want the women calling my phone, and I didn't want us to break up. I wanted things to get better, but our ups and downs were like the tracks on a roller coaster. With us, everything happened so fast, things got good really fast and went bad even faster. So, there I was at the same place that I had been so many times before. Angry that I let myself get so upset about something that I expected to happen anyway. Was I a fool for that? I guess so.

I went out to the driveway and got into his car. I had to go check up on Deidra to make sure that things were still on the up-and-up. I hadn't been over to see her in a week or so and it was about time for a visit. I never wanted too much time to pass for fear that she'd fall back off the wagon. I noticed Money hanging out on the same corner that he always hung out on. He really needed to get a life. I mean, even the small-time hustlers didn't hang on the corner all day anymore. Things had gotten more sophisticated than they were back in the day. So, I didn't understand why he still stood out there all day. I laughed as he looked over at me when I got out of the car. I thought it was hilarious.

"What's so funny?" he asked, stepping away from his post. If I didn't know any better I'd think he was a permanent fixture for the Puerto Rican store.

"You, you're always on that corner. I know your legs get tired," I said, laughing again.

"You got jokes, huh? Girl, I'm a hustler. I gotta watch my block. A lot of these young niggas will test you. I can't have my shit go up in smoke."

"Really, so you're not just trying to look cute?" I joked.

"Cute? Shit, I ain't gotta try to look cute. That shit comes naturally like that fat ass you got."

I continued to laugh at his charm. I must admit, he was pretty good-looking. For some reason it brought back memories of my crush as I was growing up. Was it because I was mad at Tyson? Hell, I didn't know what it was, but I wished that I would have sooner because he was definitely someone I wouldn't mind taking a look at every day. I laughed at myself. A girl can think some crazy things sometimes.

"Well, then I guess we are two of the lucky ones, huh?"

"I guess so, but we'd be even luckier if we hook up on some real shit."

"If I wasn't already attached to someone I would probably take you up on that offer."

"What your man don't know won't hurt him. I'm a nigga that knows how to play the background."

"Really?" I asked. I didn't believe that he could

play the background. I didn't believe that any man could. Men talk the game but as soon as they get some and start feeling you they lose control.

"Really. What, you don't believe me?"

"I didn't say that, but that's a little risky for me."

"Why, are you scared of your man or something?"

"No, I'm not scared of him, but I'm happy," I lied. I wasn't happy at the moment, that was for sure.

"It's cool, ma, I'm not trying to pressure you but if you ever change your mind you know where to find me."

He walked away and waved. Of course I knew where to find him. It wasn't like I had to go really far. I laughed again, just thinking about my earlier jokes. I would definitely keep him in mind if things didn't work out with me and Tyson. Even though I planned on staying with him, you can never really be too sure about the future. I headed to Deidra's door and knocked a few times. She peeked out of the door before taking off the chain lock and opening it.

"Girl, why don't you ever call me when you're on your way over?"

"Why? Then I wouldn't be able to catch you in the act."

"The act of what?"

"I'm just playing. What's up, though, how's the program going?"

"It's going, you know the only reason I'm going is because of you."

"I know, and I appreciate it. I just want you to get better. I need the old Deidra back," I said, laughing.

"I know, girl; don't worry, you will. I'm positive you're going to make sure of that."

I stayed over her house for about an hour before I decided to head back home. I gave Money one more wave before I got into the car. I almost thought about taking his number but I decided not to. I couldn't let temptation screw things up. It was a well-known fact that when in a relationship and things go bad we quickly migrate to someone else that can make you feel good in that time of need. I didn't want to fall victim to the risky business of having an affair. It would take too much energy. More energy than I was interested in using. Especially for a guy who lived the same lifestyle as the man I was with. He would probably do exactly the same things Tyson did. Either way, I'd probably end up unhappy and fighting to keep things stable. Was it even really worth it?

Chapter Seventeen

Diamond: Down the Aisle

I couldn't believe what I was getting myself into. Here I was about to do something that I promised myself I wouldn't do. I was on my way down to city hall to marry Kemp. Why? Shit, I'd be a millionaire if I could answer that question. We had only been together for six months, but he felt that the only way to keep this relationship together was to jump the broom. It didn't take a lot of convincing, since I wanted to keep the life that I had with him. I couldn't tell him no and risk losing him. So, the night that he crawled into bed, wrapped his arms around me, and whispered in my ear "marry me" all I could say was okay. Yeah, I might be a little crazy and even though I wasn't trying to be tied down to anyone I felt that I had to. How would I say no and convince him to stay with me? With so many women on his heels I was positive that he could pick up and leave when he got ready. I felt like the only way to keep him tied to me at this point was to marry him.

We took Kiki and his friend Black with us as witnesses. I decided not to dress up in white since to me there wasn't anything traditional about this courtship. I had always dreamed that the day I got married I would walk down the aisle with a twelve-foot train, the kind you only see on TV, and have my father standing by my side. My father, yeah, this made me think of him. I know that he wasn't my biological father but he was the only father that I knew. I could remember the day that I found out that I was adopted. I could never forget that day. I had just come home after school, starving. I had decided to play at recess a little while longer and skip lunch. As it neared the end of the day I knew that it was a mistake. I felt like my stomach was barking at my back. I ran in the house hoping that I could find a sandwich or something. I didn't even notice my mother sitting on the sofa but once I settled down I heard sobs. I looked into the living room where she was sitting with a letter in one hand and tissue in the other.

"Mom, what's wrong? Were you and Daddy fighting again?" I asked, kneeling down next to her. Fighting was something that I was used to. There had been many nights I couldn't sleep listening to them argue.

"I have something that I need to talk to you about, baby. Come over here and sit down for a minute."

"Mom, what's going on?" I didn't like the sound of what she said. I was preparing myself for the worst. Even at ten years old I knew that it didn't sound good.

"You are so special to me and I don't ever want you to think any different." She put her hand under my chin so that I could look her in the eye.

"I know that, Mom," I said, smiling. I was still trying to figure out what the hell was going on.

"Baby, I'm not your biological mother. You were adopted."

"Adopted?" I had to say the word out loud to hear it again myself. I knew what the word meant but it couldn't possibly pertain to me. How could she not be my real mom? I looked just like her or at least I had psyched myself up to believe that I did. To me, this seemed like the end. Was I being shipped away or something? Why would she be telling me this now? And what were the tears for? My mind was going a hundred miles a minute. I didn't know what to say.

"Yes, baby, you're adopted, but that doesn't mean that I don't care about you and love you like I gave birth to you."

"So what are you saying, you're giving me away or something?" A tear escaped the well of my eye. I was nervous. I thought for sure that this was the end of life the way that I knew it. Well, actually it was. It didn't matter what her answer was, my life was a lie.

"No baby, I'm not giving you away. You are my daughter."

"So why now, why did you have to tell me now?"

"Your father is filing for divorce."

"What? Divorce?" I knew the definition of this word too but I had to repeat it. I just wanted to eat. I never expected to come home to this. Just that morning my dad kissed me good-bye and gave me a long hug. Then I thought about it; the hug was longer than usual. It was as if I would never see him again. Was that the case? Was he telling me good-bye for good and not until he got off work? I got up off the floor and ran to my parents' room. I opened the drawers and found all of his empty. I looked in the closet and only saw my mother's things hanging. Did I miss something? Just the night before we had sat at the table and eaten dinner together, and today all of his things were gone and he was filing for divorce.

My mother came in the room and wrapped her arms around me from behind. I couldn't hold in the tears any longer. I wanted to leave the house, go back to school, and try this again. This couldn't be true.

"I'm so sorry, Diamond, but he's gone. He's not coming back."

"He has to, Mom, he just has to." I still didn't want to believe that what she was saying was true. I felt like I was losing it. I couldn't imagine my life without my dad. Who would fight off the boys? Who would be there to watch football with me on Sundays? That's not a mother's job. Besides, my mother wasn't strong enough to do both jobs.

I cried the rest of the night and fell to sleep hoping that I would wake up the next morning and he'd be waiting for me at the breakfast table. Knowing that I was adopted wasn't as bad to swallow, since that meant that they really wanted me if they would take the responsibility of someone else's child. I didn't care who my real parents were; it didn't matter. I wanted my daddy back. Unfortunately, my wishes would fall on deaf ears because that morning was the last time that I had seen my father. I didn't even know where to look for him. I wanted to find him and tell him that he had to come back. Sadly, I never got that opportunity.

So there I was, standing in front of this judge, Kiki, and Black, about to marry a man I didn't even know too much about. Was I afraid of losing him like I'd lost my dad years ago? Deep down did I blame myself for my father's departure? I guess I did. I had to hold on to what was mine.

The ceremony was short and sweet and we walked out of there husband and wife. We didn't even have any of our relatives there. I had never even met his mother and shit, I couldn't find mine to introduce him since she was too busy getting high. Even though I wasn't really in love, I was happy. Happy that I had a man that would marry me to keep me and one that was more than capable of taking care of me. I left city hall with a huge smile on my face and butterflies in my stomach.

We all left and Kemp took us over to Mélange, a black-owned Italian and Southern restaurant in Cherry Hill, New Jersey. The space was small and you had to bring your own bottle. Kemp had two bottle of Rosé that they put in the ice buckets for us. We talked and laughed, and I never had so much fun doing something as basic as eating. We stayed all of about two hours. The restaurant was damn near closing when we left. Black offered to drop Kiki off so that we could head home. Kemp was happy about that. I knew that he was sure to tear this up once we got home and I was ready for whatever he had coming next.

The ride home we were both probably thinking about what we wanted to do to each other. I was getting wet just thinking about it. We couldn't get to the house fast enough. I took it upon myself to reach over and rub his dick through his pants. It was getting hard just from the touch. I was horny and I wanted to suck his dick right at the moment. Fuck it, I thought, why not? He was my husband now.

I loosened his belt and unzipped his pants, releasing his dick from captivity. He looked at me shocked like he didn't believe that I would do something so daring. I didn't care, shit, even if someone saw me, I was going to lick his dick like a Tootsie Roll Pop. The pre-cum was right on top waiting for me. I loved the taste of it and I got every drop off before going down the shaft. He was trying to watch the road and me at the same time. He always said that watching me suck his dick turned him on. Shit, just thinking about his dick turned me on. If I could hop on him and fuck him while he was driving I would have.

My thick lips were wetting his dick from top to bottom. I felt his hand on the back of my head guiding me into a deep-throat routine. I loved to feel it on my tonsils and feel it beating as he moaned out loud. I was excited, which made me do a little extra, of course. I was moving to the beat of the song that played in the background.

"Damn, babe, this shit feel so good," he said in a low tone.

I was shoving every inch of him in my mouth. I didn't want to stop; it was tasting so good. Was I crazy? Did dick really taste good? Well, his did, and I couldn't wait to get home. Soon I felt the car pulling over but I knew that we hadn't reached home yet. We were still on the expressway. Kemp pushed the seat down and told me to take off my panties. I hurried up and pulled them off. I climbed over the seat and got on top of him. My pussy was already wet so his dick slid right in. I almost came as soon as it got in since it was building up the entire time I was giving him head.

"You love this pussy, don't you?"

"Damn right, I love it, it's my pussy, right?"

"Yes, it's your pussy."

"I can't hear you. I said, is this my pussy?"

"This is your pussy!" I came all over his dick. Adrenaline ran through my body and I picked up speed. You could hear my ass slapping up against his legs even over the loud music. He was holding onto to my ass cheeks tight. I knew he was about to cum. I wanted to see his face. I pulled his face close to me.

"Look at me when you bust in this pussy."

With that, he let go and his eyes rolled in the back of his head. Damn, that shit was good. I moved in to kiss him. It was a sensual kiss, probably one of the best that I'd ever had. He loved me and I felt bad knowing that I didn't feel the same way, but I was damn good at playing it off.

He started the car back up after I hopped back in the passenger seat. We headed home and once inside we had a race to the shower like two kids. He won so, I got in with him and got a little bit more before we went to bed. Well, before I went to bed, anyway. He had to go back out and work as usual. Now, what man goes out to work on his wedding night? A true hustler is what I'd call him. I didn't care about him leaving out because more work meant more money. I did want to be ready to head to the lawyer in the morning, though. Yes, the lawyer's office. I wasn't playing any games or wasting any time. I wanted to get everything signed. Shit, I had an insurance agent coming out to the house as well. I wasn't about to be married without any insurance. I might sound like a true gold digger but I simply called myself smart.

I knew what I had to do, so that the day I went through with my plan I would be able to reign over his assets the way that I imagined. I could see it now, for a change something I wished coming true. I had been unlucky most of my life with men starting with my father. I missed him and I always thought for sure one day he would come back and tell me how sorry he was for leaving me and how much he loved me. It never happened and it most likely never would. My relationships were doomed from that day. Just look at them. Johnny was in jail because I pushed him to stand up for himself. For that I was blamed. I landed in jail because of Davey and I would probably never trust another man because of the way he did me. I could partly blame myself since I let my father's leaving mold the way I reacted to men. I never wanted another man to leave me so I jumped through hoops for Davey, hoping that it would keep him with me. I wasn't about to be a fool with Kemp. I walked down that aisle confident about not turning back or ending up in the same situations that I had been in in the past.

Chapter Eighteen

Mica: Held Hostage

Where the hell was Tyson? I had been calling him for hours and he still hadn't answered. I was getting angrier by the second. He should have been here by now. I heard some footsteps near the door. I thought, *Good,* he's home. But each time the footsteps kept walking by. I picked up the phone again and it went to his voice mail.

"Tyson, where the hell are you? I've been sitting here waiting and now I'm getting worried. I know you better not be out with some bitch! Call me as soon as you get this." *Click.*

I could just scream. I hated when he promised me to go somewhere and he didn't show up. I was almost ready to get in the car and drive around until I found his ass, but I didn't want to look like a damn fool. I always thought that women were fools when they did stuff like that and here I was about to do the same damn thing.

I heard a few more footsteps then a couple of knocks. What the hell, did he lose his key? I got up from the sofa and walked over to the door. I couldn't see anything out of the peephole so I opened it. The door flew open, damn near knocking me to the floor. Instead, it slammed me up against the wall. Three guys wearing black ski masks ran in. One guy came and covered my mouth with his hand. I didn't scream because I was too afraid to. I didn't know what the hell was going on and I wished that Tyson would have been here with me.

"Where's your man at?" the tallest guy asked in a deep tone.

"I don't know," I replied. Hell, I wanted to ask him the same damn question.

"He owes me a lot of money and I need to find him. If you know where he is I suggest you tell me before you become a casualty for him." He put his gun under my chin.

"I really don't know. I have been trying to find him for hours and he hasn't answered me." I figured if I told them the truth that they would let me go. Next thing I knew he hit me over the head with the gun and I fell to the floor. I couldn't even open my eyes to see what was going on. . . .

Chapter Nineteen

Diamond: We Meet Again

"Diamond!" Kemp screamed my name through the house.

"What?" I yelled.

"I need you to do something for me, come here."

I headed down to the living room to see what the hell he wanted. I was trying to get a nap since he was out working, but I guess that was out of the question. "What's up?"

"Look, get dressed. I have somebody at the warehouse that I need you to keep an eye on. I got some shit to handle."

"Keep an eye on someone, what the hell is going on, Kemp? You know how I feel about getting involved in your mess." After my experience with Davey he knew I wasn't trying to do anything that would land me back in jail. Since the wedding three months ago, all I did was run errands. I wasn't a damn errand girl and I was getting pretty annoyed.

"Diamond, I just need you to watch someone. That's it."

"Why me, where are all of you workers?"

"They have to go with me. Come on, babe. I need your help."

"This shit better not land me in no bullshit, I mean it!" I pointed my finger at him. I reluctantly agreed to go. I wasn't trying to hear any bullshit from him. Besides, I didn't need anything standing in the way of me getting to his fortune. I wanted him to think that I would do anything for him. I needed him to believe that to get me one step closer to where I needed to be. I had already gotten him to confide in me, so believing that he had a down-ass chick was next. I put on some clothes and got in the car with him to head over to his warehouse. I didn't know what the hell was going on, but I was soon about to find out. Once we entered the building, I noticed a female tied up in a chair with her back facing the door.

"What the fuck is this, Kemp?" I asked. I was instantly pissed off that he would put me in this position.

"I said I needed you to watch someone for me. That's all I need you to do."

"Your not going to hurt anybody, are you?"

"Look, someone has stolen from me and she's my bait, okay. Just sit in here and watch her until I can free up another guy to do it for me. Babe, please do this for me," he said before pulling me close and kissing me on the forehead.

"Don't have me here too long. I don't want to be mixed up in this."

"Okay, I'll be back soon. Thanks, babe." He left

with the guy that he had sitting here before we came. I didn't know what to do or what to say. I just stood there, stiff. Why the hell was she here? I didn't really want to know. I thought about trying to make small talk, but I didn't want her to know who I was. I didn't want her to see my face in case anything bad happened and she could ID me. I grabbed a chair and sat down, still sitting in an area where her back was facing me.

"Who's there?" she asked, trying to turn her head to see me.

The voice sounded so familiar to me. I still sat quiet.

"Please, who's there? Let me go, please," she continued to plead for her freedom.

I definitely wasn't in any position to let her go. Hell, I didn't even know why she was there. I did know that I wished that I had never agreed to sit there. Her voice continued to stick out to me like a thorn. I knew that I'd heard it before, but I couldn't put a finger on it. The longer I sat there the more anxious I got. It had already been an hour and after listening to her sob and beg for an hour I thought that I should talk to her to calm her down. The whining was definitely getting on my last nerve.

"What's you name?" I asked as I still sat in the chair. I figured that I could make small talk without her seeing my face.

"My name is Mica."

"Mica?" I said, shocked. That was a name I hadn't heard in years. I knew the voice sounded familiar. How the hell did she know Kemp? Now I knew I had to reveal myself, especially if I wanted to get more information out of her. I got up out of the chair and began to head over to where she was sitting. She was squirming in the chair, probably unsure of what was going to happen next. I walked around in front of her. She looked up at me and before speaking she gave me a look of death. I knew that she'd hated me ever since her brother had been locked away. What was I to say to her? I hadn't seen her since she moved out of the neighborhood.

"Diamond? You little bitch, are you the reason that I am here?" Her eyes pierced me like a knife.

"I still see things haven't changed. I didn't even know that it was you here, so how the hell would it be because of me?"

"I've never trusted you. You've caused nothing but trouble in my life."

"Trouble? How have I been trouble?"

"Everything you touch turns to shit! My brother, me; shit, your own family gave you up!"

"First of all, my family didn't give me up and you should do your research before you speak. You don't know what the fuck you're talking about and you aren't in any position to be throwing jabs." I was pissed. Me being adopted had always been a sore spot for me and she knew that.

"Whatever, Diamond, you know that what I'm saying is true and the truth hurts, doesn't it?"

"It's not the truth so it doesn't affect me. Good try, though." I tried to blow her off, hoping that she would just end the conversation or change the subject. I hated that I had been adopted and I tried my hardest to act as if it weren't true.

"You can try and fake it but you can't hide your true feelings."

"I'm not hiding anything and since you're Miss-Know-It-All, I want to see you get yourself out of the bind that you're in!" I walked away angry. I was going to try and help her out because deep down inside I did feel bad about the way things turned out with her brother. I knew that I couldn't change any of it and I wasn't sorry for anything that I'd done. I had moved on with my life and I stayed as far away from her as I possibly could to allow her to do the same. I could see now that she still held a grudge and she probably would never shake it if she hadn't by now.

We both sat silent for a while. I pulled out my cell phone to play a game of solitaire since there wasn't anything else to do in here. I was counting every minute waiting for Kemp to come back so that I could go the hell home.

"Diamond," she called out, in a low tone. I hesitated before answering because I wasn't in the mood for anymore of her ranting.

"What?"

"Look, I'm sorry for what I said. I was just pissed off."

She sounded sincere but the way I looked at it, she could be faking just to get me to let her go. I wasn't about to do that since Kemp would have my head on a platter. If there was one thing that Kemp didn't play with it was money and since she was obviously here because of that I couldn't go there.

"And what's your point?" I rudely responded.

"Look, Diamond, we were friends at one point. We are grown women now and the way I see it we can put the past behind us and let bygones be by-gones."

"What made you change your tune? Because you were definitely singing a different song a few minutes ago," I asked, confused. Was this chick bipolar or something? I didn't know what the hell to think about her attempt at reconciliation, espe-cially since she was just putting me down a few minutes earlier. But I also had to acknowledge the fact that she'd probably say any damn thing to get out of here alive.

"I know, and that was just me being selfish. I thought that you were the one that put me here. I know that you didn't have anything to do with it now and I'm sorry."

"What makes you so sure that I didn't have any-thing to do with it?"

"Because I know you, and I know that you wouldn't do anything like that to a friend."

"Friend? Are you fucking kidding me?" I laughed.

"Yes, Diamond."

"We stopped being friends the moment that you blamed me for your father's murder," I said. I hated the fact that she blamed me for it. I could have never predicted what Johnny would do.

"I know that I blamed you but I'm over it. I was young and I didn't understand what was going on. I didn't want to lose my brother and I thought that it was your fault. I recently visited him and he told me how much he misses you. I didn't even know that he still thought about you."

"He misses me, he really said that?" I began to move back over to the chair where she was sitting.

"Yeah, he did. He said that he writes you all the time but you never respond."

"I never got any letters from him."

"He sends them to your grandmom's house. That's the only address he knows. You should probably ask them."

On the outside my expression was pretty stiff, but inside I was smiling all over. I actually thought he'd written me off like everyone else. It felt good to know that my very first love still loved me.

"So, where have you been all of these years? I never thought we'd meet again, especially not like this." I asked. I was warming up to her by now.

"Out Germantown, I wasn't that far. I guess we just hung out in different places."

"So, why are you here? Did your man steal from Kemp?"

"I don't believe that he would do that. I mean, he was loyal to him. He made sure that things were always on point. I warned him about his crew, though. They were too sloppy and if anybody stole from him it was one of them."

"When is the last time you seen him?"

"I haven't seen him in a week. I've been worried as hell, calling him all day but his phone goes straight to voice mail. I don't know what the hell is going on."

Now I felt bad for her. I was well aware of the shit that you go through for a man. I'd had many ups and downs but I knew how to keep it moving. It's a shame that we put so much trust in a man and then they leave us out to dry. Kemp was crazy as hell and I could see him blowing her away for something that she couldn't control.

"Look, I'll tell you straight up, Kemp is crazy and if he doesn't find your man I can see him hurting you."

"But I don't know where he is," she cried, probably realizing the severity of the situation.

"No man is worth dying over, so I would try every avenue I could to find his ass."

"How will I do that if he doesn't let me go?"

"I can try to talk to him about letting you go just as bait to find your man. Then you can let them square it out."

"I can't do that, Diamond. I love Tyson."

"Well, Tyson obviously doesn't love you. He knows how Kemp is and he left you out to dry," I replied, honestly. She needed to see the truth one way or another.

"I don't believe that."

"Well, if you want to die, then so be it. I tried to help you."

"I can't make it without him, Diamond. He's all that I have. I don't have any life or money without him."

"You do have a life, I learned that a long time ago when I thought the same thing. Get your mind right, Mica. You're going to die because he doesn't give a fuck! Girl, I care about Kemp, don't get me wrong, but I'm in this shit to win it. He's filthy rich and I'm trying to have it all. Fuck a man, you can do it on your own, you feel me? Me and you, we can take this shit together. All you gotta do is find Tyson for Kemp and he'll let you go. Then we can work on the master plan together." I had just thought a few minutes earlier how I could use her in my plan. Two heads were definitely better than one.

"Are you serious, Diamond? How the hell are you going to take his money? You just said how crazy he was."

"I know, but I know him like the back of my hand. I know his weak spots. We can make this shit work," I continued to pitch my plan to her, hoping she would go along with it.

She sat silent as if she was contemplating what she would do. Shit, I thought it was pretty simple. There was no way in hell I would die for a nigga. A long time ago I probably would have felt the way she did but I had grown up so much so that I knew when a man wasn't shit. Her man hadn't been anywhere to be found for a week. He'd probably taken the money and went into hiding. If he cared about her the way she thought that he did he would have taken her with him. I mean, that's what a real nigga would do but he seemed like a nut anyway.

We heard the door opening without warning. I could see the fear in her eyes. I turned toward the door as Kemp came in and headed in our direction.

"What the fuck are you talking to her for?" he yelled, probably pissed that he still hadn't found Tyson.

"Excuse me, Kemp; don't talk to me like that, okay? I did you a fucking favor!"

"Babe, you don't need to be talking to her. I asked you to watch her, that's all."

"Look, we need to talk. Can we go in the back?"

"Not right now, I need to holla at her."

"No, we need to talk. Now," I raised my tone to

get his attention. He looked at me and then looked at her. He hesitated before moving.

"Come on," he said, turning away from her and heading toward the back of the warehouse. "What is it that's so important, Diamond? I have shit to do."

"Stop acting like I'm the fucking problem, okay. I had shit to do before you dragged me over here."

"Okay, Diamond, what is it?"

"Look, I talked to her, okay? She doesn't know where he is, but if you let her go she agreed to act as bait to find him," I lied.

"Why the hell would she do that?"

"Because I told her that he ain't worth dying for."

"So she just gonna take your word and set up her man? Get the fuck out of here, Diamond, I don't believe that shit."

"Well, go ask her yourself," I instructed.

He gave me a strange look and then walked away heading back to where she was sitting. If she didn't go through with it then I could at least say that I tried. Hell, at this point the choice of life or death was hers.

"So my girl tells me you told her you'll help me find your man?" He stood in front of her. I stood in the back, waiting to hear her answer. I hoped for her sake she wouldn't be stupid.

After a few seconds, she replied, "Yes, I did say that."

"Well, I think that takes balls, sweetie, and I'm gonna let you go, but know this right here: If you try to bullshit me, I'll blow your fucking brains out."

"I won't," she said in a low tone.

I kept my silence but inside I was happy that I was another step closer to what I was trying to accomplish. I didn't think it would be that easy to get Kemp to let her go but I guess I underestimated myself. Kemp definitely trusted me and I needed to keep it that way if this was going to work.

Chapter Twenty

Mica: Seal the Deal

"Where the hell are you, Tyson? I've been worried sick." I left out the part about me being kidnapped and beaten, how they held me while they searched for his ass.

"Mica, I'm sorry. I got into some shit, okay, and some dangerous people are looking for me. I couldn't stay there; I had to go."

"Why couldn't you take me with you? You just left me, Tyson."

"I couldn't do that, Mica. I'll be back soon, though, as soon as the smoke clears."

"How do you know it will clear? What the fuck did you do?"

"I took a shitload of money from my boss. I had to; I was tired of working for pennies while this nigga made fortunes from my work."

"You really stole from him?" I asked. At that moment, I believed what Diamond said. He didn't give a damn about me. He knew that he took money from a dangerous man and he just left me in the line of fire. I couldn't believe that I had been so stupid. "Tyson, I miss you, I really need to see you."

"Maybe I can meet you somewhere, but you have to give me a chance to think of somewhere safe. I will call you back in a couple of days."

"You promise?"

"Yes, I promise. Make sure your phone stays on."

"Okay."

Days turned into weeks and I was nervous wondering when Kemp would come banging on my door. I prayed that Tyson would call me soon so I could get this over with. I wanted to move on with my life and there was no way Kemp was going to allow me to do that if he didn't find out where his money was. I barely left the house in the two weeks that had passed. Shit, even when I did leave I was looking around like I was a damn fugitive running from the police.

What the hell had I gotten myself into? I mean, when I met Tyson I thought that he was perfect in every sense of the word. He took control just the way that I liked it. He helped me and my mother out of our financial rut and kept me wearing all of the flyest clothing. Now, I could see that his greed meant more to him than I ever did and I had to make him just as important to me as I was to him, which wasn't much at all.

My funds were running low and I wasn't about

to look for a job. I had to figure out a game plan to get back on top. Besides the fact that I had grown accustomed to it, so had my mother and I didn't want to let her down. I was beginning to get depressed and I damn sure didn't want to mirror the look my mother had when my father died.

It was Friday and I had to hurry up and make the bus to go see my brother. I was determined to patch things up with him and I'd prayed before boarding that he wouldn't refuse my visit as he'd done in the past. On the long ride to the prison I continued to think about the turn that my life had taken and it was strange that I still didn't regret any of my decisions. Even though the happiness was coming to an abrupt end it was happiness that I probably wouldn't have had otherwise.

After checking in and being searched I was sent to the waiting room to be called. I was getting annoyed the longer I sat. I couldn't figure out what the hell was taking so long for them to bring him down to the visiting area. There were tons of people in the waiting area that day, most of them women probably in here to see their drug-dealing men. Shit, if Johnny wasn't my brother you wouldn't catch me dead up in here. I'd be damned if I'd drag myself this long-ass way to see a man who knew what the hell could happen if they sold drugs. The minute his ass was locked up would be the minute our relationship ended. I know that didn't sound like a woman who was in the situation that I was in right now, but there were just certain things that I wasn't going to settle for no matter how good a man was to me.

After sitting for another hour I walked up to the

window and waited in the long-ass line. Once I got up front the woman looked at me as if I was diseased or something. I didn't know what the hell her problem was but if I'd seen her on the street and she gave me the same look her ass would be hitting the floor.

"Hi, I've been sitting here for over an hour and my name hasn't been called yet. I was trying to see if there was anything going on with my brother."

"What's the name?" she asked, twisting her lip.

"Jonathan Brooks."

She looked over at the book that was on the side of her desk and looked back up at me. "What's your name?"

"Mica Brooks."

"Okay, it says here that he refused your visit."

"Refused?"

"Yes."

"Why wasn't my name called, then?"

"I don't know, I just got here."

"Does it have a reason for him refusing?"

"No, we don't ask. If they don't want to see a visitor we leave it at that."

"Are you sure that's what it says? I'm his sister; he doesn't even have any other visitors besides me."

"That's what the paper says; now could you step aside? There is a long line behind you."

I couldn't believe what I had just heard but I knew that there wasn't anything that I could do at the moment. Why the hell would he refuse my visit? What had I done? I was going through so much and now was the time that I needed him most. I wanted to cry but I held it in because I didn't want everyone in this crowded room to see how upset I was. So many thoughts were running through my head. Was he pissed that I hadn't been up to see him? Or was he upset that I hadn't responded to any of his letters? I would have to write him now since he didn't know any of my phone numbers to call me. I felt bad that I had been so distracted that I'd forgotten about him. I mean, I did have a life and I was trying to get things straight for me and Mom. I guess that doesn't matter to you when you're locked behind bars and no one seems to care about you. Most would say that it's the time when you find out about who really cares. I did care about him—hell, I probably loved him more than myself—but I still had to live and I hoped that he could understand that.

I had to wait another hour for the bus to get back to Philly and I couldn't have been more upset. I had come all the way up there just to be turned away. I thought back to the times when we were younger and how close we were. My father was the most abusive man that I'd ever known. I could remember covering my head with the pillow trying to block out the sounds of the lashes my brother received. My father would use anything that was in arm's reach, from a shoe to a chair. Anything that he could grab he would use to hit Johnny with. Now, my abuse was a little bit different. Instead of using random objects he strictly stuck to the belt-over-the-behind method with me. I guess he didn't want to leave welts and bruises all over my body for fear that someone would see them. My brother always vowed that he would get us out of there as soon as he could make enough money to take care of me. Unfortunately, the murder of our father came first. I always wished that I could turn back the hands of time beyond that day so that I could talk him out of it. Who knows if it would really work but at least it would be more than I can say that I did now. I kind of blamed myself for hooking him up with Diamond in the first place. Johnny was pretty shy and would never talk to a girl on his own. Had I not been so quick to tell her that he had a crush on her they would have never been an item.

Once I was back in Philly I caught a cab from Center City to get back home. I wasn't in the mood to catch another bus, so I would just pay whatever the cost was to bypass the aggravation of the bus riders. My phone rang just as I was a few blocks away from my apartment so I fumbled through my purse until I found it. The number was private and I usually don't answer private calls but something told me to pick it up.

"Hello?"

"Mica, it's Tyson."

"Where the hell have you been? You were supposed to call me weeks ago." I was angry because I could have been killed, thanks to him.

"I know, I'm sorry. I got caught up in some shit, but where are you now?"

"I'm in a cab about to go home."

"Look, tell the driver to drop you off down Hilltop at the store."

"Okay," I agreed. I knew exactly what store he meant and I guess he said that just in case anybody was listening. I told the cabbie to head down Lansdowne and then I did the unthinkable. Actually, I did what I had to do. I called Kemp and told him where I was meeting Tyson and he told me I better be telling the truth or he'd kill me. I was scared shitless praying that Tyson would be where he told me he would be. I couldn't imagine what Kemp would do if he got there and Tyson was nowhere to be found.

I paid the cabdriver the forty dollars it cost me for the detour and got out of the car. It was getting dark outside—it was about 7:15. The street was pretty empty besides the men who held the corners down. I hated corner hustlers—to me they would never make enough money to do anything else. I looked around nervously as the cab sped away. I held my pocketbook close to my body hoping that no one would try to rob me. I entered the store and asked the guy at the counter if Tyson was there. He looked me up and down for a second before picking up his phone and calling him. Tyson came out the back of the store and smiled when he saw me.

I smiled too. I was happy to see him though I knew that I had set him up for his downfall. I didn't say a word. I just wrapped my arms around him for what would probably be the last time I'd ever see him.

"I missed you so much," he whispered.

The sound of his voice so close to me sent chills up my spine. What the hell was I doing? How could I feed him to the dogs? This was once a man that I admired and now he was going to be out of my life. I stared into his eyes as if I was trying to read his mind. I didn't want him to let me go but I knew what was coming next.

"I missed you too," I replied, after a few seconds

delay. "Why did you do what you did, Tyson? I don't understand."

"Baby girl, you'll probably never understand it. Things are so different when you're hustling for a fucking crook. Kemp was trying to break me off with shit and I always went above and beyond. I tried to keep things basic but the longer I stayed the more I say that he didn't give a fuck about me. Kemp doesn't care about anybody, not even that fucking trophy bitch, Diamond, he carries on his arm."

"Baby, there had to be another way. I mean, what are you going to do? You can't be on the run forever."

"I know, but I don't plan to be. I just want to let things die down a little bit."

I didn't get a chance to respond before I heard the bell of the store's door opening. We both turned to look, though both of us had different reasons for it. I saw Kemp' face and I quickly moved to the side. Tyson looked like he had seen a ghost as he looked at Kemp and then back at me.

"Thought you could rob me and run away, huh? Guess you're not as smart as you think you are."

"What the fuck do you want, Kemp? I broke my fucking back for you and you never gave me what was due to me."

"Nigga, I made sure your pockets stayed fat. What the fuck are you talking about?"

"You know exactly what I am talking about," he yelled, as he stood his ground.

I was practically shaking in my boots. I didn't know what was about to go down but whatever it was I prayed that I came out of it alive. They stared each other down as I tried to get as close to the wall as I could. Without warning, Kemp pulled his gun out and shot Tyson five times, not wasting one bullet. Blood sprayed all over me, the counter, and the potato chip rack that was close to where Tyson had stood. As if five shots weren't enough, Kemp moved closer to him and pumped two more shots in his head.

"No one steals from me! I mean that shit," he yelled, before spitting on him. He looked at me standing in the corner crying. I couldn't believe the man that I had loved was gone.

"Let's go!" he yelled, grabbing me by the arm. I didn't say a word. I just did as I was told. I thought for sure that I was next. We got inside of a black Yukon where there were two other men inside. I had blood all over my leather jacket, face, and hair. Kemp got in the driver's seat and drove off.

"You all right, baby girl?" he asked as he sped up the expressway.

I didn't respond. I couldn't respond. What the hell was I supposed to say? I just saw him blow away the love of my life. He was my everything and now I was going to be forced to fend for myself. I mean, I was glad to be alive but I wasn't glad that things had to be this way. I had hoped that there would have been a way that they could have worked through their differences so that I could have my life back, but I guess Kemp did what he had to do.

Kemp continued the drive to the unknown destination since I had been too afraid to ask where he was taking me. Soon, we pulled up in front of an apartment building. I was still staring out of the window thinking about what I had just witnessed. The sight played over and over in my mind. All I could see was Tyson's body falling to the floor.

"Get out," the slim thug sitting next to me spoke while nudging me.

I did as I was told and slid out of the car. Kemp got out of the driver's seat and grabbed me by the arm, leading me to the apartment entrance. He unlocked the door with a key, swung it open, and pushed me inside.

"Look, you can stay here as long as you need to. I know you probably won't be able to pay the bills at your man's place alone. I'm going to send somebody over with some clothes so you can change. You're gonna have to lay low for a little while. That asshole said my name so I'm sure the cops will be looking for me."

I still didn't speak. I sat down on the sofa and listened to what he had to say. What else could I do? I was stuck here whether I wanted to be or not. Kemp wasn't the kind of guy that you wanted to test.

"If you try to turn me in you'll end up like your man, so I'd suggest you go along with what I say. I'll be back later on tonight, in about an hour or so someone will bring you the clothes, so open the door."

"Okay," was all I could say. I still had tears running down my face. He glanced back at me before walking out of the door. I broke down once he was gone. I know Tyson wasn't the perfect man but he was all that I had. I was sorry now, but it was too late to make a difference. I know that I had no other choice since I would have been dead. Kemp proved that he would kill so I wouldn't have stood a chance. Tyson's murder had sealed the deal, and now I had to figure out what I was going to do next.

Chapter Twenty-one

Diamond: Together Again

"I need you to take these clothes over to the apartment on Wayne Avenue," Kemp said, passing me a stack of women's clothing.

"What bitch you got over there that I'm dropping clothes to?" I replied, putting my hands on my hips.

"The chick I had you watch before. Her clothes are all bloody so I need you to take these to her."

"Bloody? What the hell did you do, Kemp?"

"I handled my business, that's all you need to know."

"Did you kill somebody?" I asked, as I began to tremble. I was afraid to hear the answer to the question.

"You don't need to know all of that, Diamond. Stop with all the questions and just drop the damn clothes off."

"Excuse me, I'm your wife, I'm entitled to know what the hell you've done."

"No, you don't. I'm not going to argue about this shit, Diamond. I got other shit to do."

"I'm going to take them but this conversation isn't over."

"Whatever," he responded, heading up the steps, leaving me standing there with the pile of clothing and a question mark above my head. By his reaction I knew that he killed someone and since Mica was who I had to drop the clothes off to I figured that it was her man. I had to come up with what I was going to say to her. I could definitely use her if I was going to get the money I was trying to get. I didn't feel bad about it since she had shut me out of her life years ago and blamed me for something that I had no control over. For me she was just an added bonus and another part of my plot. She was someone to cause a distraction for Kemp and at this point he still didn't know that I knew her. For now, that's the way I wanted to keep it.

I got in the car to head over to the apartment where he had stashed her. She probably was all bent out of shape and needed a shoulder to cry on. I wasn't really into all the emotional shit but I would have to fake it to get her to trust me. I had built up a wall after being hurt so many times that it was hard to break. Nowadays you had to be that way 'cause a weak heart is only going to get stepped on. The one thing that I cherished was my sanity and I wasn't going to let anyone take that away from me. It took me all of fifteen minutes to get there. I took a deep breath and got ready for my performance before using the key to enter the apartment.

When I opened the door she jumped out with a knife. She got pretty close, almost stabbing me. I moved out of the way just in time for her to fly right past me.

"What the hell are you doing?" I asked, grabbing hold of her arm so she could drop the knife.

"I'm trying to protect myself. I thought for sure he was sending someone here to kill me," she cried, as the tears flowed and she dropped the knife on the floor.

"Trust me, if he wanted to kill you, you'd already be dead. Here, he told me to give you these clothes."

"I don't understand. He killed him right in front of me and he's going to just let me go?"

"Obviously, you're still here."

She sat down on the sofa and buried her face in her hands. She cried out loud, probably wishing she were dead. Her life was going to be different now whether she wanted it to be or not. I sat down next to her and placed my hand on her back. Appearing to be supportive was the first step to gaining her trust.

"I'm sorry, I hate people to see me cry. I've never been this scared before in my life. I don't know what to do."

"All you have to do is listen, I'm going to get you out of this."

"How are you doing to do that?"

"I told you that day at the warehouse I had a way that you can have your own money and your own shit without a man. I meant what I said and I'll guarantee that things work out for you."

She didn't respond. I wondered what was going

on in her mind. She probably still didn't trust me, but I knew that I could work my way up to that. After about a minute of silence she got up and headed to the bathroom. I sat still on the sofa. I heard the shower running so I took that time to call Kemp and let him know what was going on.

"Did you get there yet?" he asked in an annoyed tone.

"Yeah, I did, what the hell is wrong with you?"

"Nothing you need to worry about. What is she doing in there?"

"She's taking a shower. She's just upset but I'm trying to get her together."

"All right, well hurry up and get back on this side, it's getting late and you know I don't trust these niggas."

"I'm leaving in a few minutes."

"All right, I'll see you later."

"All right," I said, before ending the call. I sat on the couch and flipped through the TV channels waiting for her to get out of the shower. She came out of the bathroom dressed in the clothes that I had brought over. I wondered where the hell Kemp got the clothes from in the first place. They damn sure weren't mine. I didn't even wear sweat suits. He probably got them from one of the tricks he deals with on the side. I didn't ask any questions because I didn't feel like arguing.

"I didn't think you would still be here."

"Where did you think I'd be?"

"I don't know. I don't know anything right now, I feel like I'm flying on autopilot."

"Look, I didn't leave because I wanted to make sure you didn't need anything before I left. I gotta get back home because it's getting late. I'll be back in the morning to check on you. Get some rest, all right?"

"I'll try. Am I really safe here?"

"Of course, I wouldn't leave you if you weren't." I continued to lay it on thick. I had her right where I wanted her to be.

"I really appreciate this. I know I don't deserve it for the way that I treated you and some of the things I've said."

"It's okay, we can talk about this tomorrow. You've had a traumatizing day so go to sleep and I'll see you in the AM."

"Okay," she said, while reaching out her arms for a hug.

I instantly felt uncomfortable. I wanted to play it off but I didn't want to be so affectionate. I loosened up once I quickly thought about how good things would be for me once this was all over with. I leaned into the hug and headed toward the door. After making sure that she locked up I got in the car and headed back home. I wasn't surprised that Kemp wasn't home. He was rarely home; he normally got in around three in the morning. I never really worried about where he was because the bottom line was that if anything happened to him, I was going to have everything. Shit, they would be saving me time and effort if they got to him first. I did care about him, don't get me wrong, but not the way I cared about men in the past. I wouldn't allow it.

After getting home and changing I jumped into bed. I probably was asleep as soon as my head hit the pillow. I had an exhausting day, both mentally and physically. From the outside looking in you'd probably wonder what the hell was so exhausting about shopping and living the lavish life. Shit, it took a lot of work to maintain my looks. I had to have the best of everything. Living at my grand-mom's was hell. I had to share clothes and shoes. Getting out of that neighborhood was the best thing that could have happened to me. Once I got a taste of the good life there was no turning back. I didn't care what people thought about me. I was smarter than most people thought I was. Every-thing I did was calculated, and there wasn't any turning back.

Besides the steady drug business that Kemp ran, he owned property from North Philly to Chel-tenham. He owned a barbershop, a small-car dealer-ship, and two restaurants. Being his wife had its perks, and I sucked every ounce of it up. I stood to inherit it all, plus the money that he had stashed away in a safe. He told me everything and that's the reason why I married him. There wasn't any way I was going to mess up. See, some people talk too much and that was his problem. A little bit of pillow talk goes a long way. He trusted me more than he should and that was going to be his down-fall.

I woke up when he climbed into bed at two-thirty but easily went back to sleep. I woke up around nine the next morning and he was gone. I hadn't even felt him get up. I did wonder why the hell he was up so damn early. He never got in the bed until the afternoon. I dialed his cell phone but he didn't answer. Forget it, I had plans for the day anyway and I wasn't going to let him ruin them. I took a quick shower and got dressed. Within an hour I was on my way back over to check on Mica. Isn't that what friends are for? I cracked myself up.

Once I got there I noticed Kemp's car in the lot. What the hell was he doing there? I hope I didn't have to go in here and act a fool. It was too soon for this, I didn't need her to get his attention this quick. I needed more time. I used the key to open the door. Kemp was talking on the phone but I didn't see Mica in the living room.

"What the hell are you here for?"

"I was about to ask you the same thing," he replied, ending his call.

"I came here to check on her, I told her that I would. Now what's your excuse?"

"Same, I had to check on her to make sure she ain't try to run out on me."

I didn't believe him but it didn't matter, what you don't see won't hurt you, right? Well, at least that's what I was brought up to believe. I looked around the apartment to see if things were out of place. Everything pretty much looked the way that they did when I left last night.

"Where is she at anyway?"

"She's in the room 'sleep. I was on my way out but I had to make a phone call first. Good looking out, though, maybe you can keep her occupied so she don't do nothing stupid," he said, before getting up out of the chair and heading over to where I was standing. He grabbed me and hugged me. I returned the affection but it was hardly genuine. I knew he wasn't telling me the absolute truth but I couldn't really feed into it if I wanted things to go right. I could have played the wife role and come in there having a fit but what would that have accomplished? Kemp and I would have argued and Mica probably would have never trusted rekindling our friendship. I had learned not to be too nonchalant but I had also learned not to take things overboard. He kissed me on the cheek before he headed out of the apartment.

I set my bag down on the table and walked into the bedroom where Mica was still sleeping. I stood there and stared at her. I know that it was a really weird thing to do, but it gave me a little time to think. First, I thought about the fact that I planned to willingly use her to entice my husband. Now, that could go either way. Kemp was extremely good-looking and with all of the money he had, most girls would wait in a line ten city blocks long just to get next to him. She could end up falling for him and letting him know what I had planned. That would probably land me six feet under, a place that I wasn't trying to visit any time soon. Next, I had to think about the possibility of him finding out that both of us was trying to set him up and he'd end up killing both of us. Last, I had to evaluate the fact that he could end up surviving, leaving us both in the danger zone. Was it all worth it? I asked myself a million times, but then I remembered my grandmom's house and the way that I used to live. There was absolutely no way that I was going back there. I mean, I knew people who lived in worse situations. I could have been living in one of those abandoned houses, I could have been living with a pedophile, and I could have been in so many situations that I've known others to be in but I wasn't. Yes, my mother was on drugs now, and that was something that I was going to fight tooth and nail to change, but it still wasn't as bad as it could have been.

Regardless of all of that, I wasn't going back to North Philly. I wasn't going to school and I damn sure wasn't going to get a job. So, what other choice did I have? Was I supposed to stay married to him, as controlling as he was? Was I supposed to keep doing his dirty work and end up in jail again? Was I supposed to really fall in love and make a bunch of babies? Hell no! None of the above was going to happen. I came up with the plan and I was sticking to it.

I had just turned around and was on my way back out to the living room when she woke up.

"Hey, you made it back over, I'm glad you came," she said as she sat up in the bed and began rubbing her eyes.

"I told you I was coming, and I'm a woman of my word."

"So, what do you have planned for today?"

"Well, I was going to suggest that we go out to the mall or something."

"I don't know if that's a good idea since Kemp told me I need to lay low for a while."

"Girl, he doesn't make the rules for me. What's the point of keeping you locked up in this apartment? That makes you look suspicious, if you ask me. You need to live your life as you normally would."

"I'm just afraid."

"Listen, trust me. He's my husband so I know

him like the back of my hand. He'll probably be a little pissed but he'll get over it."

"Okay, but I don't have any other clothes but these."

"We'll take care of that, now hurry up and clean up so we can go. It's nice outside too, girl. I'm gonna let the top down on the convertible. I'll be waiting for you outside."

I left the apartment to go out to the car. I felt like I was on my way to the top. There wasn't anything else in the world that would give me the ultimate satisfaction. I was smiling from ear to ear as my hair blew in the spring air. It was a beautiful day and I was dressed to kill in a little black dress and wedges. Everything was perfect and I was a firm believer that everything happens when it's supposed to. I was meant to be a boss and I had no doubt that I was going to succeed. Mica and I were back together again as friends and this time it was going to be worth my while.

Chapter Twenty-two

Mica: New Horizons

I was relieved that I was still breathing. I had never been so thankful for something in my life. I thought that I would never be able to be happy if I wasn't with Tyson but now I saw things a little different. Yeah, I was silly and a fool in love but how many of us aren't at one time in our lives? Since he gave me a life that I wasn't accustomed to I thought that staying with him was the only way to keep it. I wasn't stupid by a long shot—I was just stuck in that mind-set. Though I hadn't been close to Diamond in years, at one point in time she was my best friend. Honestly, I knew that she wasn't responsible for my father's death but I had to blame someone in order to come to grips with the fact that he was gone. I could never blame my brother because he was the only person in this world that I loved more than myself.

I had to live my life and I wasn't going to sit

around depressed about the past. I'd be damned if I was going to end up like my mother. So, I had a new outlook on life and thanks to Diamond I was about to find out how to make it in this world alone. I would never have to depend on a man again. I thought my brother would be proud of me. I knew that he would be happy that I was going to be friends with Diamond again. He never stopped loving her, even after not having contact with her for years. There had to be something special about that.

I hurried and got dressed, excited about our outing. I was ready to show everyone the new me. Though Kemp was a ruthless murderer, he did have a heart and I got a taste of his heart this morning when he came over. He sat down and talked to me and apologized for tearing my life apart. I never expected him to be so nice. I thought for sure that he didn't have a heart. I knew that what happened had nothing to do with me but I also knew that he had to handle his business. He still didn't want me to leave the apartment just yet and he still warned that if I told anyone what happened he would have no choice but to get rid of me as well. I promised that I wouldn't and we shook hands on it. I fell back to sleep and by the time I woke up he was gone and Diamond was there.

I opened the door to the bright sunlight. It was nice, Diamond definitely hadn't exaggerated. She was sitting in her car blasting the Jay-Z *American Gangster* CD. I was a huge fan of Jay-Z so I was surely going to enjoy the tunes mixed with the spring air.

"So, what mall are we going to?" I asked, as I

stood outside of the passenger side of the car. She hadn't even heard me walk up, she was so into the song that was playing.

"You'll see, hop in so we can get out of here!"

She continued to sing along with the music as we headed through the street to the expressway. By the look of the roads she was taking it appeared that we were going to the King of Prussia Mall. I could go crazy shopping in any mall, but that mall was definitely my weakness. With so many stores, I could shop for hours and not miss a beat. I was ready to run through the mall like a kid in a toy store. I sat quietly on the ride just enjoying the moment. Before long, we were pulling into a parking spot and she was closing the top of the car.

"Don't worry about any money, girl, I got you covered. You can grab whatever you want."

"Thanks, Diamond, you don't know how much I appreciate this," I replied. I really did appreciate it because I couldn't go back to Tyson's place and I didn't have any clothes or enough money to start over.

We hit almost every store you could think of. I tried on clothes while she sat in the waiting area and vice versa. She promised me a night out on the town to have some fun, so I was desperate to look my best. I grabbed shoes and bags. I got makeup from M•A•C and lingerie from Victoria's Secret. I was set from top to bottom with clothes. The only thing left was to get my hair and nails done and I would be set. She spent more money on me than I probably would have spent on myself.

I had to evaluate a few things, though. Was all of this kindness genuine? Or was she just using me as a pawn in her little game? I would hate to think that but I didn't have a choice. For some reason, the longer we hung around each other at the mall the more I started to believe that it was all a facade. I mean, she seemed to be overly nice, which made it a little difficult to be optimistic. Either way, I was going to go with the flow for now. If she were up to something, it would come to light sooner or later anyway. In the meantime, I was going to enjoy myself because I deserved it. After shopping we decided to get something to eat at Friday's. I hadn't eaten all day and it was almost four o'clock before I realized it. I'm surprised that my stomach wasn't growling. There wasn't a wait so we were seated immediately. I was a picky eater so there wasn't much on the menu that I would order. I decided to keep it basic and get some chicken fingers. I figured that you couldn't go wrong with that. I hadn't had a drink in a while either so I ordered an ultimate margarita. If you're familiar with Friday's then you know that the ultimate drinks come in a big-ass glass. They tried to fool you because there wasn't much in these glasses than a regular glass. The deception went with the thickness of the glass, making you believe that you were getting a whole lot more for a few more dollars. I figured that out a long time ago. I still got them just because if I didn't I would be tempted to order more and me and alcohol don't mix well at all. I'd done some crazy things when I was drunk and would wake up the next day and not know where the hell I'd been or what the hell I'd done. I didn't know how to stop when I'd reach the point of no return. So, my method was to psych myself out, thinking that I drunk a lot when I really hadn't. It may sound silly but it worked for me.

"So, how is your mom doing? I haven't seen her in so long," I asked, trying to make conversation.

"My mom is strung out, girl; you probably wouldn't know her if you saw her."

"Are you serious? Damn, I'm sorry to hear that. Do you remember my cousin Deidra?"

"Deidra . . . Yeah, I remember her. What's up with her?"

"She was messed up on drugs too but I finally got her into a rehab and she's doing so much better now. Have you tried to get your mom into a program?"

"She's hard to find and when you do find her she doesn't stay long and she will tell you she's not going to a rehab. I don't know what else to do so I see her when I see her and I give her a few dollars and keep it moving. I got my own problems; I can't be chasing her around. Shit, she's a grown-ass woman," she spat, as she dug into her salad.

Damn, I thought, that was cold. I knew how hard it was to get a drug addict to a rehab but that's what you do for your family. How could you just give up on your mom like that? I decided to change the subject since I could feel myself saying something that would most likely cause an argument.

"Is that all you're going to eat?" I asked, looking at her soup and salad. She had a perfect figure so it wasn't like she needed a diet or anything.

"Yeah, this is pretty much all I eat, girl. How you think I stay this size?"

I laughed, since I knew she would say that. It's always the small chicks that swear they need to lose some weight. I was happy with my size-eight frame.

"So what's up with your mom? Last time I saw her y'all were packing up a U-Haul truck," she asked.

"She's doing okay now, but she was depressed for years. Shit, I had to get a job to help her with the bills because she couldn't handle them alone. I feel like I never got a chance to be a kid. I don't regret helping keep us afloat, but I wished that my father would have been alive to take care of us. That's why I fell in love with Tyson, because he kept my mom straight." I got sad just saying his name. I was definitely going to miss him.

"I know you miss him, girl, but you'll be okay. Women are born to survive tragedy. Just like you took ahold of the situation when your dad died you'll do it again. Don't ever feel defeated, because it's not becoming. You'll never get anywhere in life like that. Believe me when I tell you I've been through some things but I never let any of it get me down. I kept it moving and I won't stop until I get enough. You feel me?"

"Yeah, I know exactly where you're coming from."

Okay, now I had a newfound respect for her. What she said was so true and I believe that I once felt defeated. I had actually felt that way on more than one occasion. From the time I sat and begged my brother not to shoot and watched him pull the trigger. Or the time that I was forced to lose my virginity and I kept it to myself. Or when I focused so much of my attention on a no-good man that I forgot about my family. I had lived a lie for these last few years of my life. Tyson couldn't love me the way that I loved him and it wasn't until that very second that I realized it.

"I learned a lot from my last relationship, girl. I had to sit in jail for nine months for some shit that he got me into. After that shit, I promised myself that I would never ever love a nigga more than I love myself. It's not feasible for me. Fuck getting a nigga with money. I'm about getting a nigga but I need my own money!"

"I know that's right!" I agreed. Everything that she said made perfect sense. You had to be a fool not to understand it. "I can't believe that you went to jail, that shit is crazy, girl. What happened?"

"I really even hate to talk about it but in a nutshell, he sent me over to Jersey with drugs to drop off and the nigga I was supposed to meet up with set me up. I was sick, girl. I thought I was gonna lose my fucking mind. When I got out, I saw him and he tried to apologize. It wasn't that much apologizing in the world. I never wanted to get wrapped up in his world. I loved him too much and I would do anything for him. Each time he talked me into doing something it was worse than the time before. I don't know if he was testing me to see how far I would go or what. The bottom line was that I had to walk away or end up in jail for murder because I was surely ready to blow his ass away!" She laughed, trying to bring humor to a serious situation. I didn't know what I would do in jail—she was definitely stronger than I would ever be.

"You're strong, girl, I couldn't have survived!"

"A girl's gotta do what a girl's gotta do!"

I smiled at that comment. She had grown so much mentally to a level that I wanted to reach. I guess you have to experience something devastating to learn and to overcome it. I had learned a valuable lesson today and I was going to hold onto it for life. After we finished eating we got back on the road. All the food I ate along with the one drink had me ready to take a nap. Before I knew it I was snoring. I woke up just as we were parking at a day spa.

"Hey sleeping beauty, let's go get our nails done."

"Okay," I agreed, trying to focus. That nap was much needed I hadn't slept that good in weeks. We were treated like queens in the salon. The Asian culture was definitely serious when it came to business. They treated you so good you almost never wanted to leave. I enjoyed every minute of my foot massage, pedicure, and manicure. I hadn't been that relaxed in a while. We were in there all of an hour and change before we left to head to our final destination, the Dominican hair salon.

I came out of there looking like a new woman. I damn near didn't recognize myself. On the way back to the apartment Kemp called her cell phone. I was surprised that he hadn't called all day.

"What? . . . She's right here . . . I took her shopping, Kemp, she couldn't stay in there with no clothes . . . Who are you yelling at? . . . I hear you . . .

I just said I hear you, Kemp . . . I'll see you when you get there then . . . Good-bye!" *Click*.

"What did he say?" I asked nervously. I knew he wouldn't be happy about me coming out of the apartment.

"He's only talking shit, he's mad, but trust me, he'll get over it," she replied nonchalantly. She wasn't afraid but I sure as hell was.

"What is he going to do to me?"

"Nothing, don't worry about him. All you need to worry about is getting ready to hang out and party tonight. I'll take care of him, trust me," she reassured me.

"Is he coming to the apartment?"

"No, he's going home."

We pulled into the lot of the apartment building within a few minutes of her ending the call. She walked me into the apartment because I was afraid that he would have someone waiting in there for me. She was cracking up the whole time. I didn't think anything was funny. I had witnessed first-hand how he handled business. After opening the door she checked the rooms.

"Okay, there is no one here. Satisfied?"

"A little. What time are you coming back?"

"Be ready by ten."

"Okay, I'll be ready."

"Come behind me and lock up."

I followed her and put every lock on the door. I didn't want him to catch me off guard. I should have told her to call me and let me know what he said. Hell, she couldn't call me—she didn't even know my cell number. I did a quick search of the apartment myself. I looked under the beds, in the closets, I even checked the shower. I couldn't get comfortable till I was absolutely positive that he wasn't there. I had just got on his good side so I hoped her game was as good as she said it was. If not, I would have to hope for a miracle, praying that he would forgive me for going out when he told me not to.

My view of a new horizon was slowly getting dim. I needed confirmation that it wasn't a big deal. I decided to take a bath to calm my nerves but first I had to pin-curl my hair since I'd just got it done. The steam from the hot tub would ruin it. I put on some smooth R&B, dropped some bath salt in the water, got in, and relaxed. It was just what I needed. I planned on being ready at ten, and I was going to turn heads tonight. I had a new attitude and tonight was the premiere.

Chapter Twenty-three

Diamond: Hook, Line and Sinker

I couldn't wait to get home. I was doing damn near sixty MPH on neighborhood streets. If there was one thing that I couldn't deal with it was a man thinking he ruled me. I was a grown-ass woman, and it was about time he realized it. He was not my superior, he was my husband and that didn't mean he could disrespect me. I got out of the car and walked fast toward the door. I opened it and Kemp was in the living room with his best friend, Black. I didn't have a thing for dark-skinned dudes but I swear he was the finest dark-skinned man I'd ever seen in my life. He had bright white teeth and some juicy-ass lips. He looked like he could do some things in the bed. Anyway, back to the problem at hand. I walked straight in and interrupted their conversation.

"I need to talk to you, now!" I pointed toward the kitchen so Kemp would follow me. I was on fire and ready to explode. He got up from the chair, gave Black a devilish grin, and followed me out of the room.

"Yo, what the fuck is your problem?" he asked as soon as he stepped over the threshold of the kitchen.

"No, what the fuck is your problem? How dare you call me out of my name? I am not now nor have I ever been so degraded. I am your wife, not some trick you're fucking on the side. Don't you ever do that shit to me again."

"Are you finished?"

"No, I'm not finished. I'm upset. I can't believe that you did that."

"Babe, I was mad because you know I told her to stay in. I'm not saying I was right for disrespecting you, but she can fuck shit up for me."

"First of all, keeping her in hiding is gonna seem suspicious. What the hell is she on the run for? If the cops want to talk to her, so what, she ain't gonna tell them nothing, Kemp. She's too fucking scared. She had me checking the closets and shit to make sure you didn't send nobody there to kill her."

"Word?"

"Yes. You can't leave her stuck up in that apartment. What's wrong with her hanging out with me?"

"You know I don't trust people and I don't want to have to murk her, but I will if I have to."

"Listen, she's not going to mess up."

"Look, I'm sorry for what I said, okay?"

"You should be."

"Do you forgive me?"

I didn't answer. I was still mad but I admit I had a weak spot for a man begging me for another chance. He moved in to hug me but I didn't budge.

"Stop being so damn stubborn and give me a hug," he said, grabbing ahold of my arm and pulling me close to him. "I'm sorry, okay, for real, I won't do it again."

I hugged him back. "I'm taking her out to the club tonight. She needs to get out and have some fun."

"All right, what club? I'm coming out too."

"Solo. What, you trying to spy on me or something?"

"Come on now, you know better than that. I just want to go out, buy a couple bottles, and have some fun. Is there anything wrong with that?"

"Naw, it's cool. Make sure you have those bottles poppin'!"

"Most definitely." He slapped me on my ass as I was walking out of the kitchen.

"Watch that, you gonna get yourself in trouble." I laughed.

"Trouble? Yeah, whatever!" He joined in the laughter.

Black looked at us and shook his head. He was probably thinking we were crazy as hell. We weren't crazy, we were married and all married couples have their ups and downs. I had figured out how to stand my ground when it came to men. Kemp was a ruthless killer but when it came to me I could always get him to back down. I was still mad about what he'd said but I let it go once I thought about all the money and power I'd have once he was gone. I smiled at Black before going upstairs. He smiled back at me but played it off with a laugh when Kemp noticed him looking at me.

I knew that dealing with Black was out of the question—for now, anyway. Hell, once Kemp was out of the way I could deal with whomever I chose to. Yeah, I had my eye on him but isn't that how men work? Was it wrong to be attracted to him? I didn't think so. It was harmless.

I got dressed in record time. Kemp and Black were still sitting downstairs playing *Madden* on the PlayStation. I had on a tight-fitting sateen black dress with spaghetti straps. The top of the dress was shaped like a corset so my breasts were popping out of the top of it. My ass looked perfectly round and my shoes were animal-print wedges with a gold buckle on top. I didn't expect them to still be here but, hey, and least I could get a man's opinion on my outfit before going out.

"So, how do I look?" I said, turning around so they could get a 360-degree view. Kemp barely looked but said I looked good. He was too busy in the damn game to pay me any attention. Black, on the other hand, had his eyes glued to me like a magnet. He didn't say anything, at least not ver-bally; his expression said it all for him. Satisfied, I kissed Kemp and left the house.

Mica was ready once I got there. I was glad that I didn't have to sit and wait. I hated to be dressed for hours waiting on someone and they are fresh to death when we get in the club because they just got dressed. Kiki was good for that. Oh, shit, Kiki. I had gotten so tied up with Mica that I hadn't talked to her all week. I didn't know if she was working tonight or not. I felt bad; Kiki and I normally talked every day. She was probably worried about me and here I was trying to swindle Mica.

Once we got to the club, the line was ridiculous. I was glad that I never had to wait in lines. I knew pretty much every security guard at the clubs so they always let me skip the line. The music was on point and it was full of players and wannabe video chicks. I mean, why does everyone think they're a model? MySpace has really gotten some people confused. I scoped the club trying to see who was there. I didn't see Kiki, so she must have been off or hadn't gotten there yet.

About an hour after I got there, Kemp and his crew made their grand entrance. I saw all the hoes running up to give him a hug. It didn't bother me until one of them was hanging on him a little too long. I grabbed Mica by the hand and walked over to where he was standing to make my presence known. I wasn't trying to go to jail again but I would whoop someone's ass for messing with my money.

"Hey babe," I said, hugging him and making sure I flashed my four-karat wedding-ring set. The girl turned her nose up and waved good-bye. I returned the gesture, adding a middle-finger move.

"You're crazy, you know that? That's why I fucking love you," he laughed. "Now let's go to the VIP and get these bottles poppin'."

The VIP was crazy packed. There were some local celebrities in there along with some basketball players. We were drinking Moët like it was water. We were dancing and having tons of fun. I stepped out for a minute to go check my makeup in the ladies' room. I ran into Black on the way.

"You're looking extra sexy in that dress tonight. I had to let you know since your husband didn't," he said, looking me up and down, licking his lips like he wanted to eat me. Shit, I wouldn't mind getting my salad tossed by his fine ass. Too bad he was Kemp's best friend, because I would have given him a piece.

"Thanks," I said, keeping it simple.

"Don't get too drunk you might end up in somebody else's bed," he laughed.

"Oh, I won't, trust me."

"Just warning you," he said, smiling, and walked away.

What was that about? He might as well just come out and said he wanted some. I wouldn't have said yes, but damn, we're both grown and he could have kept it funky with me. I went into the bathroom and fixed my makeup while getting strange looks. I tipped the lady who gives you the paper towel and grabbed some gum out of her basket. I went back out and pushed through the crowd to get to the VIP room in the back. I was getting pulled in too many directions by different men but I managed to get my arms free each time. I still hadn't made it through yet, but felt a grip too strong for me to get loose.

I turned to find out who it was because I was just a few seconds away from snapping and smacking the shit out of somebody. Could these men be that ignorant that the only way to get a girl's attention was to grab her? What has happened to the days of the mack or smooth operators? Once I realized that it was Black, a little bit of steam wore off. He didn't say anything—he just pulled me close with my back facing him and made me dance with him. Was he crazy? Kemp was just a few feet away and here he was grinding on my ass. I was drunk as hell so of course I moved to the beat of the song. After the song was over, he turned me loose. I went back into the VIP section as if nothing happened. Realistically, nothing did happen but you never know how other people would react.

Kemp was drunk as hell, he was even dancing and that was extremely unusual. I joined in the fun. I noticed Black coming back in, standing off to the side making sure I was in full view. I was putting on a show, dancing all around Kemp like he was a stripper's pole. I continued to make eye contact with Black and for some reason I was getting turned on. Kemp was going to be in for a treat when we got home. I just hoped that he wouldn't get too drunk and fall asleep on me. When I was drunk I was always horny. Half of the time, Kemp wasn't even home so I had to play with my toys or just go to sleep and forget about it. A girl needs that hunger to be fed sometimes. I was always too afraid to go out and get me a piece on the side. Kemp knew pretty much everyone in the city, so any little slipup could screw up all of my plans.

Mica was enjoying herself too, dancing and rubbing up on one of Kemp's friends, JB. I was glad to see her loosening up because being depressed wasn't attractive. I couldn't stand a woman laying up worrying about a man. Even though he was dead and hadn't just stepped off, the way he was acting he probably would have left her ass eventually anyway. Mica was the kind of girl that was cute but she was the only one that didn't realize it. She always had low self-esteem and though she may not have realized it, it was true. If a guy paid any attention to her she always wondered why. I mean, how hard is it to look in the mirror? There were a lot of women who wished they had her looks. I thought it was pathetic, but it was something that I could definitely use to my advantage.

Soon, the lights were coming on and people began to disperse into the streets. For some reason I didn't feel right. I guess you could call it women's intuition but I knew that something was about to go down. I heard arguing from a distance. It was a mixture of men and women's voices. I grabbed Mica's hand to pull her down the street toward the parking lot. She was busy trying to look back and see what was going on. Being the wife of a drug dealer I learned to keep it moving. I was not interested in a fight—hell, niggas don't fight anymore, they shoot first and ask questions last.

"Mica, come on girl, let's go!" I yelled, continuing to tug on her arm.

"Girl, I'm trying to see what's going on."

"Unless you want to get shot you better come on."

The more I tugged the more she moved away, and I was ready to leave her ass. If she wanted to be stupid it would be her funeral, not mine. I started to walk a little faster and within a few seconds I heard her heels as she ran to catch up with me. We hadn't even made it to the car before gunshots erupted. I got down on the ground and pulled Mica down with me. I knew that some shit was about to go down and I was glad that I didn't stick around close to the door. I heard people screaming and scattering all over Delaware Avenue. After a few minutes the shooting stopped and seconds later the crying started. I peeked around the side of the car to see who was hit. I saw someone that resembled Black lying on the ground. Oh shit! I thought, where the hell was Kemp? I got up off the ground and began to run over to where he was. Kemp came flying around the corner with his gun still in his hand.

"Kemp, what the fuck happened?"

"Diamond, go home," he yelled. Even though I had ulterior motives for being with him I was glad that he hadn't gotten shot. I mean, I hadn't found out everything that I needed to know. It was too soon and losing him right now would just ruin everything. Kemp and his friend, JB, bent down and picked Black up off the ground. He was still alive but blood was pouring out of him like a faucet. I didn't know what the hell had happened but I prayed that Black would make it through okay. They ran toward Kemp's truck and placed him in the backseat. It was like a scene from a movie and as many times as Kemp hollered at me to go home I didn't budge. I was stiff. I thought about Black's family and his children. What if he didn't make it through this? Kemp walked over to me as JB got in the driver's seat of Kemp's truck.

"Diamond, get in the car and drive the fuck home! I mean that shit." He pushed me toward Mica.

Tears began to fall from my eyes. I was scared. I didn't know what happened and I knew that I should have listened but I couldn't. I was almost frozen in that spot. Mica came behind me and grabbed me by the arm. Kemp stared at me as he backed up to get in the car. Once he got in the car JB pulled off. I watched them drive away and hurried to the car. The cops swarmed the area. There were two dead bodies in the street around the corner on Spring Garden Street. The cops gathered any witnesses and questioned them. I told them that I hadn't seen anything, which I really hadn't. I was given a card with a number to call if I remembered anything. We left the scene and I drove home quietly. Mica agreed to drive home with me and stay until I heard from Kemp.

Once we got in the house we sat on the sofa. I turned on the TV and laid my head back to rest it on the back of the sofa. I dozed off without even realizing how fast the time had passed. It was almost seven o'clock in the morning when I realized it. Mica was on the other end of the sofa asleep. I got up and dialed Kemp's number. I knew he hadn't come home and I didn't have any missed calls so I knew he hadn't called. It took a few rings for him to answer it.

"Babe, what's going on? Why didn't you call me?"

"I'm still at the hospital, Diamond, I'm sorry. Black is still in surgery. They said he should make it out okay."

"That's good to hear." I felt a little relieved that he was going to be okay. I knew that Kemp wouldn't tell me anything more especially over the phone so I didn't pry for any more information. I knew that he wouldn't be home anytime soon so I went back to sleep on the couch. In my mind I knew that whatever beef they had wouldn't be over but I was satisfied that Black was alive. All I could remember is seeing his body lying on the ground, still. I could imagine a chalk outline on the ground tracing the spot where his body had been laid out. The good thing was that it was only in my imagination.

Chapter Twenty-four

Mica: Sucka for Love

I woke up with a pain in my neck. I wasn't used to sleeping sitting up on a sofa so I was suffering for it. Last night's excitement was a little more than I'd expected. In all the years that I had dealt with Tyson I'd never witnessed anyone being gunned down. Besides my father, I didn't even know anyone who had been shot. Was this the life that I wanted to continue with? I didn't really know the answer to that question and I knew that it didn't really matter since I didn't have a choice. Diamond was still sleeping on the other end of the sofa. I couldn't imagine being in her position. I mean, I would love the money, the jewels, and the power but all of the other shit that came with it was for the birds. I wasn't really trying to have to duck from bullets each time I went out for a night of fun. I got up and headed upstairs to use the bathroom.

For the first time, I got a chance to look around

their house. It was definitely like something in a magazine. I walked toward the end of the hall and pushed open the door that led to their bedroom. The bed was huge with posts on each end that almost reached the high ceilings. The linens were beige and cream, which matched the wood of the bed and hardwood floors. There was a huge area rug with the same colors in it. I moved close to the bed that was perfectly made. I could tell Diamond's side of the bed from Kemp's by the items neatly placed on their end tables. I bent down and placed my nose close to the sheets and could smell cologne. I wasn't crazy but I needed to at least imagine that it was my place. Even though it hadn't been that long since I was with a man, it was long enough for me to feel lonely.

I peeked in the drawers to find everything folded perfectly. Who the hell had time to organize things like this? I mean, both of them were pretty busy so unless they never touched any of these things they had to have a maid. After awhile, I felt like I was intruding too much and I would have been too embarrassed if she walked in there and caught me snooping around. I left out of the room and just as I was walking into the bathroom Diamond was coming up the stairs.

"Hey girl, you were knocked out down there. I was looking for a washcloth so I could wash my face and stuff," I lied, because I was almost caught coming out of her room.

"Oh, they are right in the bathroom closet behind the door."

"Okay, thanks, how are you feeling?"

"I'm okay, girl, just stiff as hell," she laughed, as she rubbed the back of her neck.

"Did you hear anything about Black?"

"Yeah, I talked to Kemp. He said he was still in surgery but was expected to make it out of it okay."

"That's good. Well, could you drive me back to the apartment today?"

"I thought we were going to hang out for the day. I'm stressed, girl, I need some company."

"Okay, we can hang out. What did you have planned?"

"I wanted to go shopping but I also wanted to stop by and see my mom. It'll be good for her since she hasn't seen you in years. I know she'd be happy to see you."

"That's cool, I'm gonna freshen up and if you drive me by the apartment I can change and we can hit the road."

"You can wear something of mine. You're not too much bigger than I am and I got tons of shit I haven't even worn yet. When you're done in there just look in my closet and grab whatever you want."

I was glad that we were getting back on track. I hadn't really had a lot of friends that I could hang out with. I missed it and I felt like things were going to happen for the better. I thought about last night, before the shoot-out and how much fun we had. JB seemed like someone I could get used to. He wasn't as fine as Tyson was but he was definitely more attractive with the money he had. I know it sounds like something a gold digger would say, but I wasn't a gold digger by a long shot. I was just used to a certain kind of lifestyle and the only men that I was attracted to were men that could help me keep it up. I had my eye on him and I was going to try and get any information on him that I could.

After freshening up in the bathroom, I went back into Diamond's room where she was now in the master bathroom taking a shower. I opened up the double doors that led to her huge walk-in closet. There was so much to choose from, I didn't know where to start. I'd never seen so much designer shit in one place in my life. I had been treated well by Tyson but he'd never spoiled me like this. I took down different articles of clothing and put them close to my body, modeling in the mirror. I felt like a kid in a candy store. If there was one thing that I loved, it was to dress up. Normally, I didn't feel like I was pretty or desirable. I always needed someone to tell me that I looked pretty and even then I still didn't believe it. Putting on one of her outfits would definitely boost my confidence and a little boost was just what I needed. I settled on a black Betsey Johnson dress. It was a casual dress and would work perfectly in the spring air. I put it on and it fit perfectly. How Diamond and me ended up the same size, I'll never know. I was always a little thicker than her especially in the thigh and booty area but over the years she'd filled out in the areas where she was once lacking.

She came into the room and looked at me with a smile. I stood there waiting for her approval.

"Good choice, I love that dress. It looks good on you," she said.

I was relieved. For some strange reason I felt like I needed to hear her say those words to me. I was desperate for attention and I was going to try my best to be as perfect as possible. I knew that was what I had to do if I wanted to snag a hustler. Diamond quickly got dressed and put on her makeup. She looked as if she was ready to go walk a runway, definitely not like she was going to pay her mom a visit.

Once we got into her two-door convertible Mercedes-Benz, she let the top down. She turned on the radio and instantly began singing along with the popular Beyoncé tune "Get Me Bodied." I did like the song, so I started singing and dancing along with her, quickly forgetting about the wind and my hair.

Driving through the old neighborhood brought back so many memories. Even though it wasn't the best neighborhood it was what I called home. I didn't know anything better existed until I met Tyson. All I knew were abandoned houses, drug dealers, and fiends. The streets were filthy but we skipped and ran all around them as if they were invisible. I smiled inside, thinking of being a kid again. Having my brother to watch my back and keep me safe. Though my dad was abusive, I missed him. What girl wants to grow up without a father? There were a lot of things that I didn't get a chance to learn from him. I was forced to fend for myself when my mother's depression turned her into a shell.

Soon I turned my attention off of the sad things and focused on the good. At least I made it through okay because there were plenty of people that had fallen victim to the same society that I grew up in. We parked in front of her grandmother's house. I laughed because everything looked exactly the same. Even after the years passed she still had the same lawn chair on her porch and a bunch of flower-pots hanging around the awning. Diamond looked at me, probably wondering what the hell I was laughing at but I straightened up when she turned back around. She walked up to the door and began to knock. It took a few seconds for someone to open the door.

"Diamond?" her aunt asked, as if she wasn't sure who she was. I knew that she didn't come down here very often, but damn, how could you forget your niece. I soon realized that she did know who she was but was just startled by her visit.

"Why are you acting like you don't know me?" Diamond asked, turning her face into a frown. She was clearly annoyed.

"I'm not, Diamond. I'm just surprised to see you, that's all," Cicely replied, still holding her spot blocking the door.

"Well, the good thing is that I didn't come to see you or else I would've been crushed by the warm welcome," Diamond replied sarcastically. "Where is my mom?"

"Your mom?" Cicely asked, still playing dumb. I didn't know what the hell was going on here but I could tell that there wasn't going to be a happy ending to it.

"What's up with you today? I don't think I'm speaking in another language."

Cicely stood there silent as if there was some-thing that she wanted to say but just couldn't muster up the courage to say it. What the hell was going on? Now I was curious. Diamond was becoming more agitated and soon she pushed her way past Cicely and went into the house. She stood there staring at me as if she wanted me to do something. What was I supposed to do? I didn't even want to move from the step that my feet were planted on. I heard Diamond in the house calling her mother's name over and over again, then I heard her grandmom call out her name from a distance. I assumed that she was upstairs because I heard the sound of Diamond's shoes on the hard wood. It was so strange because I was still standing on the steps and Cicely was still standing at the door with a blank look on her face as if we were stuck in time or something.

Within a few minutes Diamond came flying out of the house, pushing Cicely out of the way and heading toward the car. She had tears streaming down her face. I didn't know what to say.

"Diamond," I called out to her. She didn't turn around to face me.

"Let's go!" she yelled in response.

I ran to the car and got inside. I could barely close the door all the way before she was speeding off down the street. She was crying hysterically, wiping her eyes to make sure that she could see the road.

"Diamond," I called out her name again.

"What?"

"What happened?"

"If I had a gun I would shoot that bitch! I mean, I knew that she hated me but she took this shit to another level."

I sat there quiet, still confused. I didn't know who or what she was talking about.

"My mother is dead," she cried.

"Dead?" I asked, confused.

"They buried my fucking mother and didn't even tell me. How could they do that shit?"

"They did what?" I had to ask again to make sure that I was hearing her correctly. Who would do that? I mean, you would have to be a real fucked-up individual to neglect to tell someone their mother died.

"She died, Mica, she fucking died and they didn't bother to tell me." She stopped at the light and put her head down on the steering wheel. I put my hand on her back and tried to quietly let her know that I was there for her. I knew how it felt to lose a parent and it was something no one wanted to experience. She probably felt bad since her relationship wasn't as close as she would have liked it to be. The reality of that is once they're gone you can never get the chance to make up for the time that was lost.

The light turned green and the cars behind us started to beep their horns. She wasn't in any condition to drive so I told her to pull over so I could take over from there. She did and I was glad that I didn't have to argue with her to do so. People rarely make the best decisions when they're upset and I wasn't trying to be a casualty of something that I didn't have any part in causing. She got out and walked around to the passenger side, glancing at me before getting inside. I didn't know what to say so I stayed quiet. What could you say at a time

like this? Nothing that I said would make her feel
better or come close to bringing her mother back.

I figured that we would just go back to her
house and get in contact with Kemp to let him
know what had just happened. She continued to
sob as I made it down the expressway toward
their home. I made sure to glance at her every few
minutes to make sure she wasn't having a nervous
breakdown or anything like that. Shit, that was the
last thing that I needed to happen right now.

We pulled up to the house about a half hour
after leaving her grandmom's house and the driveway was empty, which meant that Kemp wasn't
home. Damn, where was your man when you
needed him? She got out of the car once I parked
and walked like a zombie up to the front door. I
followed behind her.

She went upstairs and within a few minutes I
heard the bathroom door close and the water
began to run. I wanted to ask her for Kemp's number so that I could call him but I'd leave that decision up to her. If she wanted to call him I figured
that she would have called him herself. Since she
didn't, I would mind my business and relax downstairs until she came back down. A few minutes
later the phone rang and startled me. I let it ring a
few times before I answered it. It was strange that
I felt comfortable enough to answer her phone,
but deep inside I was hoping that it was Kemp so
that I could tell him what happened.

"Hello," I said in a low tone. I didn't want Diamond to hear me.

"Who is this?"

"Mica. Is this Kemp?"

"Yeah, where's Diamond?"

"Something bad's happened, she needs you right now."

"Bad? Like what?"

"I'll let her tell you when you get here but she really needs you right now."

"All right, I'll be there."

Damn, that was easy, I guess he really did care about her. I didn't expect him to just drop everything and come right home. Men like Kemp usually cared more about their work and money more than anything. I'm not saying that they're heartless but their priorities are just different than normal people. The shower was still running, I thought that it was pretty long for her to be in there but I figured that she was using it to drown away tears. I had done it myself in the past and though it wouldn't make everything go away, it eased the pain temporarily.

About twenty minutes later Kemp came in the front door. He looked at me, probably waiting for an answer, but I sat quiet.

"Where is she at?"

"In the shower, she's been in there a long time, though."

He ran up the steps skipping two at a time. I heard him banging on the bathroom door and calling her name. I began to get worried so I hurried up the steps and stood at their bedroom door. She wasn't answering and his knocks got louder and louder. After a few more seconds of no response he used his shoulder to knock the door open. I ran to the bathroom to follow him. Diamond was sitting on the floor of the shower with the water running over her. She was awake but had a blank stare on her face. This is what I was afraid of. Kemp shook her a little bit and called her name. She still didn't respond. Kemp picked her up and brought her out of the bathroom. I grabbed some towels and put them on top of her.

"Babe, what's going on?" Kemp asked, as she began to come out of whatever trance she was in. "Talk to me, Diamond."

"I'm okay, I was just a little tired."

"No, that was something else. What the hell is going on?"

"Her mom died and they didn't tell her," I blurted out. She gave me an evil stare, but shit, he needed to know. She was acting crazy. I didn't know what the big deal was. Why wouldn't you want your husband to know what happened?

"What? They didn't tell you?"

"No, they didn't. I was a little upset but I'm okay now. Honestly, I just want to be left alone so I can go to sleep."

"You sure?" Kemp asked, while rubbing her hand. This was the sensitive side of him and strangely it was turning me on. I mean, Kemp was fine as hell and not to mention super rich. What woman wouldn't be turned on by him?

I stepped out of the room to give them some time. It wasn't long before Kemp came downstairs and joined me on the sofa.

"Is she okay?" I asked.

"I guess so. That's fucked-up, what her family did."

"I know, I couldn't believe it, I just stood there trying to figure out what the hell was going on."

"Well, she's the type that likes to hold shit in until she explodes, so if she doesn't want to talk she won't."

"I'm glad that you came though because I was almost on my way out the door." I lied. I just wanted to make him believe that his presence was appreciated. Shit, his wife damn sure wasn't.

"It's cool, ma, I'm so used to her; it don't even bother me anymore."

"Well, it should. I mean, she *is* your wife." I sat still, wondering what his response would be.

He turned and looked at me puzzled, probably wondering where the hell that came from. I mean, he didn't know our history so he couldn't possibly think that we were friends. I was glad that she'd been helping me out but I still didn't trust her and at this point she shouldn't trust me, either. Her man had caught my eye, and if she wasn't willing to do what she had to do to keep him I was going to let him know that he could find what he needed in me. Hell, I was a sucka for love and any way that I could get it I was planning to.

Chapter Twenty-five

Diamond: Stick to the Script

Though I was still angry, I realized that I didn't have a choice but to get over it if I wanted to move on with my plans. I didn't trust Mica as far as I could throw her and I almost doubted her importance. I mean, did I really need her? I didn't doubt that I could handle it on my own, but now that she knew a little bit of what I had planned she could potentially ruin it all. I wasn't about to let that happen. I felt like she was trying to backstab me anyway. I didn't ask her to call Kemp nor did I ask her to tell him what happened so I knew that she had an angle. I just had to figure out what the hell it was.

I tried to steer clear of her for a few days just to get my plan in order. I decided to let Kiki in on what I'd been up to. I hadn't spent much time with her lately and I knew that she would probably think I was crazy, but I was far from crazy. I was more determined, if anything. I lightly knocked on Kiki's door, hoping that she wouldn't peek out the door, see it was me, and leave me standing there like a fool. I stood out there for a minute or two and had turned around and began to head back down the steps. I heard the lock on the inside turning and smiled as I turned back around.

"Still impatient, I see." She laughed, while putting her hand on her hip and shaking her finger at me like I was a student that had been bad in class. She was right, I was impatient and I'd probably always possess that character trait.

"I know, girl. I missed you; I thought you would be pissed at me."

"I am pissed but it doesn't mean I'm not happy to see you," she said, reaching out to give me a hug. "Where the hell have you been?"

"Long story, girl," I said as I walked into her living room.

"I'm listening. Shit, I want to know what had my best friend so tied up she couldn't even call and see how a bitch was doing."

"Kemp got me wrapped up in some crap." I conveniently left out the fact that my mother had died. I didn't want her to feel sorry for me so I figured the only way to do that was simply not to tell her about it.

"Don't tell me you're going down that road again, you promised me you wouldn't do that to yourself again."

"Hell no, girl. I'm not a damn fool. I know better than to get wrapped up in that again. You remember that girl Mica I told you I used to hang with back in the day?"

"I think so, but what does she have to do with anything?"

"Well, Kemp kidnapped her because her man stole some of Kemp's money. To make a long story short we started catching up on time lost and I felt like I could use her in my plan."

"Plan? What the hell are you talking about, Diamond? I don't know if I like the way that sounds."

"Well, you know that when I met Kemp my goal was to get enough money to make it on my own. I wasn't trying to get caught up like I did with Davey's trifling ass. I only made it official and married his ass because I could get so much more from it. I'm about to get what's mine. Shit, I've been through too much pain not to."

"I'm still clueless."

"I'm going to take over Kemp's empire."

"What?" she asked, before bursting into laughter.

"What's so funny about that?" I was a little annoyed—laughter definitely wasn't the reaction that I was expecting. I expected her to be upset and try to talk me out of it. That was the Kiki I knew. Even though what she said usually went in one ear and out of the other I still liked to hear it from time to time. At least that made me think that someone cared about the choices I made, because the reality is most times I didn't. I know that may sound like the dumbest things you've ever heard, but it was just the way that thing were. I've made a lot of decisions that were careless, but I usually came out on top.

"It's not really funny. I just can't believe you're serious, but if you are I want to know how I can get a slice of the pie."

Now I was really confused. What the hell had happened to her in the past month? "Kiki, are you serious?"

"Yeah, girl, shit, if you're going to hit it big why can't I join you? I am your best friend, unless Ms. Mica has come and taken my place."

"First of all, I don't even trust her so there is no way in hell that she could take your place."

"So then tell me about the plan and stop beating around the bush."

"Okay, I have to get rid of him in order to inherit all of his businesses and money."

"What? What the hell do you mean, you want to kill him?"

"That's the only way." She probably really thought I was crazy now.

"You are really serious. What's gonna happen if you get caught?"

"I'm not going to get caught; I'm way too smart for that."

"Being smart ain't got shit to do with it, the smartest people get locked up. I just hope that you know what you're doing because I don't want to see you in the penitentiary."

"That's not even an option."

"Well, you know I got your back and anything that you need me to do I got you."

She reached out to hug me. I was confident that she had my back no matter what. I wanted her help but I knew that there was a possibility that I would get caught. I didn't want to drag her into my mess. I was afraid of going to jail again, especially for murder, but I had to go through with it. Was I crazy? Maybe a little, but who wouldn't want to inherit all that I stood to gain? There wasn't anything that I wanted more than the power of running his empire.

"I love you, girl, even though you're crazy as hell!" She laughed.

"I know." I joined in the laughter.

After leaving I stopped at the Hallmark card store to pick out a get-well-soon card for Black. He had left the hospital and was in rehab. I hadn't gotten to see him since the night of the shooting. I called Kemp to see where he was, since I didn't really want him to know that I was visiting Black. Was there a reason for me to leave that information out? Definitely, since no man wants competition and I'm sure that if he had any competition in the world Black was the strongest contender. It took me all of a half an hour to find the perfect card. I wanted to make sure it said all I wanted it to say. I was just on my way out of the store when my cell phone rang. I took it out and glanced at the caller ID. It was Mica. I really didn't want to talk to her, but I knew that if she knew I was angry it would screw things up.

"Hello?"

"Hey, girl, what's going on? Feeling any better?"

"Yeah, I'm okay."

"What are you doing? I want to go to the mall."

"I have to make a run, but if I get done early enough I'll call you."

"I can make the run with you if you stop by and scoop me up."

"No, I'll see you when I'm done. This is something

I have to do alone." I was getting annoyed. I barely wanted to talk to her ass, let alone hang out with her at the damn mall.

"Okay, then, just call me. I'm bored to death over here."

"All right," I quickly responded before I hung up. I was trying to hurry her off the phone before I made it to the rehab. I didn't want her to hear anything in the background that would give her a clue about where I was. I still didn't trust her and I still hadn't figured out what trick she had up her sleeve.

Once I reached Black's room I was almost too nervous to go inside. I didn't know if I should have been there or not. I definitely couldn't risk Kemp finding out about the visit so I was planning to make it quick. I knocked on the door even though it was open and smiled when he turned around to look my way.

"Diamond, what's up? I'm surprised to see you here."

"I know. Glad to see you're up moving around," I said before passing him the card and bending down to give him a hug. The hug felt so good that I almost didn't want to let go. He obviously didn't want to let go because each time I tried to pull away he pulled me closer. It was weird but it was something that I wanted. Shit, I wanted more but I knew that now wasn't the time to pursue it.

"This feels too good, I don't want to let go," he whispered into my ear. The whisper sent chills up and down my spine.

"Well, I can't stay here forever so I guess that means you have to."

"I guess so," he laughed. "So what brings you here? I'm surprised Kemp let you come up here unsupervised."

"I didn't tell him that I was coming."

"Why not, you plan on doing something wrong?"

"I don't plan on it but shit happens."

"Shit happens, huh? That's your excuse for wanting me?"

"What excuse? And who said that I wanted you?"

"Come on now, Diamond, we're both grown. You don't have to bullshit me. I'm a real nigga and I know when someone wants the kid."

"I'm happy with Kemp so I'm really not trying to screw that up."

"You're not happy and we both know that. You need a nigga like me in your life. Kemp has the money and power but you'll never be much more than a trophy to him."

"What?" I was a little annoyed by that comment, but honestly it was probably the truth. Was I nothing more to him but a prize to put on display? The fact that I was using him should have meant that I didn't care, but it didn't. Who wanted to feel used? I definitely didn't take that kind of thing lightly. "I doubt that I'm his trophy. I am his wife. Why would he have married me in the first place?"

"Because that's what he does. You're not his first wife, Diamond. Kemp likes control and by marrying you he can keep you closer. You fell right in line like the other ones just because of the dollar signs."

"He's been married before?" I asked. I couldn't believe that he hadn't told me that. I should have known by the way he rushed me to get married.

Damn, I hoped that didn't mean I would have competition when it was time to collect the money. I wished that I had known about this from the beginning.

"There are a lot of things about Kemp that you don't know. He's pretty good at keeping secrets. I've known him all my life so I know more about him than anyone."

"So why are you telling me this?"

"Because I like you and I feel like you deserve better."

"But if Kemp found out you know that he would be furious. Why would you risk that?"

"Kemp doesn't scare me and when I've got my eye on the prize I fight to win it."

I had to really sit back and think about what he was saying. Was he really serious? How the hell would he expect to be with me with Kemp still alive? I couldn't let him know what I planned to do, but it was weird that he would come at me as if he already knew. I know that I was smarter than most women and definitely smarter than the other wives he had. I knew this because I was his wife now. I'd be dammed if I was going to let him walk away from me and leave me with nothing.

I was tempted to let the inevitable happen. Black knew that I was attracted to him and it was just a matter of time before I let myself fall for him. But then my plan came back to mind. I couldn't mess it up—I had to stick to the script for things to go my way.

Chapter Twenty-six

Mica: Make Me Love You

If she even had the slightest clue that we were sneaking around behind her back, I'm positive I'd have a fight on my hands. I couldn't resist. Following the night that her mother died I was there for him when she wasn't. We had formed a bond and he promised me that soon I would be able to take her place. Besides the fact that I didn't trust her, I knew for a fact that she was using him and he was a good man, for the most part. He had his flaws as did everyone else, but I'd rather have the man and the money and not the money without the man. What was I supposed to do? Turn down a man that could make all of my dreams come true? I was a sucka when I fell for Tyson but Kemp was different. He was a man of his word. I knew for a fact that whatever he said he would do—would be done.

I thought about my brother a lot lately. I still

hadn't been able to see him and even letters telling him that I was friends with Diamond again didn't get me a visit. I didn't know what else I could possibly do to make him want to see me, but I wasn't about to give up on him, either. I decided to try one last time to visit him. If he turned me away this time I wasn't going to force myself to try it again. I took the long ride up to the prison and was searched and put into the waiting area. After waiting for a half hour my name was called. I smiled. He hadn't turned me away. I rushed toward the door that led to the visiting area. He sat there at the table with his head down. Either he was tired or not happy to see me. I didn't care, at least this time he accepted my visit.

When I reached the table he looked up but didn't speak. Almost as if he didn't have anything to say or was waiting to see what I would say first. I had a lot to say, so much that I didn't know where to start. He looked different as if he'd aged five years since the last time I'd seen him. He stood up, silent, and reached his arms out to give me a hug. He was thin, not the muscular body that I was used to.

"I'm glad to see you," he said in a low tone before sitting back down in the seat.

"What happened to you? Are you sick or something?"

"Damn, it's that obvious?"

"What's wrong, Johnny?" I began to get nervous. I could tell by looking at him that something was wrong but I wasn't sure if I was really ready to hear his answer.

"I'm sick, baby girl, real sick," he said without looking me in the eye.

"Well, what is it? What's going on, Johnny?" I could feel the tears building up and I knew as soon as he told me they would begin to fall.

"I have cancer and I don't have much longer to live."

"Cancer?" I asked to make sure that I heard him right.

"Yeah, I have cancer and I want to apologize for not accepting your visits. I was being selfish because I didn't want you to see me like this."

I couldn't speak. The words were sinking in. I was going to lose my brother and there wasn't anything that I could do about it. After the shock came the anger. I was upset that he had denied me the time. His time was limited and he hadn't even thought about how this would affect me, especially since I hadn't been able to see him in months. I wanted to tell him the things that had been happening, but after hearing what he just said I felt like it wasn't even important. Besides, I didn't want to upset him. I was still crying. He reached across the table and held my hand.

"I'm sorry, Mica," was all that he could say to me. There wasn't anything that would make me feel better. I wanted to hear that this was all a big joke or a bad dream. I wished I could turn back the hands of time and he wouldn't have been here in the first place.

"I can't believe this, Johnny. Does Mom know?"

"Yeah, she knows, but I told her that I wanted to tell you myself."

"So she knew all this time and didn't tell me?" I was furious. That was just like my mother to with-hold information. I didn't care if he'd told her not to tell me, how could she think it was okay not to tell me that my only brother was dying?

"I'm sorry, Mica."

"Stop saying you're sorry, it's not your fault that you're sick. I just wish you would have told me sooner. Here I was thinking that you just didn't want to see me. I knew that I hadn't done anything wrong but that's how I felt. Horrible."

"I was trying to protect you."

"Protect me from what? I was going to have to know eventually." I didn't care what the reason was. It didn't matter if I found out now or six months ago, I would still be just as upset as I was. He'd always tried to protect me and protecting me was what got him locked away in the first place. Protecting his little sister was what he was sup-posed to do but with him it had always been to the extreme. He would always fight for me—he didn't care how big a person was or how hurt he'd get. I still remember the beatings that we got from our father. I could see the look on Johnny's face as I stood in the corner for hours after a beating be-cause I couldn't finish my dinner. My father's tem-per was uncontrollable and the smallest thing would set him off. Unfortunately, the traits we hated the most about our father were passed on to Johnny and he'd die thinking about it.

"So, enough about me, let's talk about you. What's happening in your life?"

"Nothing that I want to talk about." I was still stuck thinking about what he'd just told me.

"Listen, Mica, you can't let this get you down. You're a soldier. I'm gonna be all right and think about it this way. At least I won't be locked up anymore. Anywhere's got to be better than here."

He was right, any place would be better than prison but that idea still wouldn't make me feel better about the fact that he would be gone soon. Eventually, I opened up and was able to tell him a little bit of what was going on with me before the visiting time was over. I told him that I had a new love in my life but conveniently left out the fact that he was a married man. I also left out all details concerning Diamond. I didn't want to risk anything upsetting him. I had a lot to think about on the way back. I was glad that I'd finally got to see him and know that there wasn't anything that I had done to make him upset with me, but I was still upset about losing him.

I decided to go to Diamond's to see if she felt like shopping. I called a cab, which arrived about a half hour later. If I'd had a choice I wouldn't go with her but I didn't have any friends. I know that's pathetic but it was the truth. I was never able to form any close friendships especially after I fell out with Diamond. I got to the house and didn't notice her car in the driveway. I still decided to knock just in case she had put it in the garage. I stood there for five minutes or so before I heard footsteps.

"What's up?" Kemp asked, standing shirtless. I almost melted right into their welcome mat. He smiled, probably noticing the trance that he'd put me in.

"Is Diamond here?"

"No, but you can come in; she won't be here for a while."

"Are you sure, Kemp? I don't want her to walk in here and catch me here with you."

"She's not coming anytime soon, trust me."

I hesitated but decided to take the chance and go for it. Hell, I couldn't resist him when he was fully clothed, so looking at him half naked was like a magnet. He closed the door as I walked toward the living room. Before I knew it he was hugging me from behind. I could smell his cologne as it tickled my nose. He must've taken a bath in it for his skin to smell as good as it did.

"Kemp, what are you doing?"

"What do you mean? You know what I'm doing." His hands were steadily caressing me. I still tried to push him away. I was nervous. I had already had a bad day and I didn't want to risk her coming in here flipping out. Each time we'd met it was at the apartment. I had never been so bold to come in their house to meet up with him. Kemp didn't care one way or another since he was looking for a reason to leave her. I, on the other hand, wasn't in a rush to get into a confrontation. The way I was feeling, I couldn't stop him from making me feel good. I wanted it, I needed it, and I was sure that it was going to be worth it. He hadn't let me down yet. Besides his money and looks, I knew firsthand why all the women fell for him and he did too. He used his instrument to his advantage and that advantage was to make you love him.

He moved me toward the stairs as he continued to caress me and kiss my neck. I didn't fight it, instead I let him guide me up the stairs to the bedroom. *The bedroom.* I thought I was finally going to get the chance to lie in the bed that I'd imagined. I remembered the first time I came in the room and wished that it were mine. I was closer to that dream than ever and nothing could make me see it any other way now.

His lips were making a path down my back and sending chills all through my body. My panties were soaking wet, anticipating feeling him inside of me. I wanted to be with him, I wanted to love him. He moved me closer to the bed and bent me over before palming my ass. I held the position, ready for what he'd do next. He raised my dress and pulled my panties down. I assisted by stepping out of them and getting back in the doggy-style position. I didn't even hear him dropping his pants, but I knew that he had once his dick was rubbing up and down my wet pussy. I almost came early but I held it in. He pushed me down on the bed and pulled my ass up a little then entered me from behind. His dick was thick and filled me up. I was moaning loudly; this was even better than I had imagined. Diamond didn't deserve all of this. She wasn't in love with him. I wanted to prove that she couldn't love him like I could.

Once he turned me over I took the initiative to push him on his back. A man loved when a woman took control, became aggressive. I straddled him and looked him in the eyes. I moved up and down then into slow circles, grinding my hips so that his dick could go deeper. He was moaning with me. At this point, I couldn't hold in my eruption any longer. My juices began to run down the shaft of his dick, making it extremely wet. I was sweating, he was sweating, and I was going wild trying to reach another orgasm before he reached his.

"Oh shit, oh shit, damn, I'm cumming, oh this pussy is so good!" he moaned.

I felt myself reaching another orgasm; again, I came all over him. I was exhausted but satisfied. I stopped and looked at him. He smiled. I hoped that this wouldn't be the last time we were together. I wanted this to last for a very long time. The problem with that was, it wasn't up to me. God had his own plan. I heard a click as if it were a gun pointed in my direction. I jumped off of Kemp and found Diamond standing at the door with the face of evil. I didn't know what to say, how could I explain this?

I almost went numb as Kemp tried to reason with her and calm her down. It didn't matter, she had her mind made up. Now, instead of me being able to share in the wealth, she was going to kill me too. I had betrayed her, she trusted me. I should have thought about it more before I jumped into their bed. I should have planned this better. Maybe had I told him what she planned to do I wouldn't be sitting here facing a gun. I couldn't even move, I wanted to just close my eyes and imagine that it was all a dream.

It wasn't a dream and the two bullets that hit me confirmed that. All I felt was burning, then wetness, and then I felt dizzy. I couldn't move, I felt my eyelids getting heavy and I couldn't hold them open. I felt pain and then nothing . . .

Chapter Twenty-seven

Diamond: HBIC

Two months had passed since the night that I'd killed Mica and Kemp. For at least two weeks I couldn't close my eyes without replaying the scene. I could still see the blood splattered all over the room. I was sick for days and even the help of Kiki and Black couldn't get me through the funeral. If you'd been there you would have thought I deserved an Oscar, but honestly it wasn't a performance. I couldn't bear to see Kemp laid up in a casket. Not because I loved him and was sorry for what I'd done, but because I couldn't get the scene of the murder out of my head. As for Mica, I didn't go to her memorial because I felt that there wasn't any need to act as if I cared. It may sound cold, but that was just the way it was.

I had inherited all of Kemp's assets, including the two-million-dollar insurance policy that I had on him. His stores, his cars, his homes—everything he had was all mine and there wasn't anyone who could take it from me. His drug empire—well, that was mine too and I know some would wonder how a woman could do a man's job, especially a man with as much respect and power as Kemp. It was pretty simple—since they respected Kemp, they respected me. That may sound foolish because Kemp was dead, but it didn't matter and just as they worked for him they now worked for me. Maintaining order was the easiest part, keeping my feelings for his best friend a secret was the hardest.

Yes, I admit it, I've loved Black since the moment I saw him. I always believed that if this had been another lifetime, I would have been with him a long time ago. I didn't really know how his workers would take to me starting a relationship with Kemp's right-hand man, so I held off as long as I could. It didn't take long before I couldn't resist and his advances didn't make it any easier.

Black had stepped up, helping me run things. I would have never expected him to do that for me. Especially after I found out that he knew about the fact that I killed Kemp. Yeah, I was shocked when I found out too. I wondered how the hell he would know and I was also nervous because I believed that if he knew then that meant there could possibly be someone else that knew too.

Going back to that night, I thought that I had covered everything but obviously I hadn't. The night that he told me, I sat across from him still as a statue wondering how I could have been so stupid.

"I saw you when you left the house with the

trash bag in hand. You had on a sweat suit and I've known you long enough to know that you wouldn't be caught dead in that getup. Plus your face looked strange, like you were upset. I was going to say something but I watched instead. Once you left, I went inside and saw the scene, then I knew what happened. I threw some stuff around to make it look like a robbery gone wrong and I bounced."

I continued to sit still. I thought for sure he would have reported me to the police. I mean, Kemp was his best friend.

"Don't think I'm going to turn you in because I've already incriminated myself. Shit, they'd lock my ass up with you. I don't know what happened in that room and at this point, I don't even want to know."

"So you put you freedom in jeopardy for me?"

"Actually, I did it for us. I see opportunity here. What would you going to jail prove? That I'm a snitch? Naw, I'm far from being a snitch, I'm a businessman. I wanted you for a long time and what better time than now, to make that happen?"

"Are you serious? What the hell would the workers say? They'd think we set the whole thing up."

"No they won't, this makes perfect sense. Why go out searching for a good nigga when you have one right here in front of you?"

Okay, I guess he was serious. What he said made sense. I probably wouldn't find a man that could deal with my newfound wealth nor one that could hold it down for me. What was I supposed to do? I needed some help. Fuck it, I was going for it. I got up out of the chair and kissed him. He kissed me back. I was ready to tear his clothes off and fuck him right on top of the desk. It had been a few months since I'd had some. Our lips unlocked; he stared at me as if he was thinking what I was. I was about to walk to the door and lock it when I heard a knock. The door opened.

"Girl, what's up?" Kiki said, holding a bouquet of flowers. "These were outside on the step."

"Outside?" I asked. Black looked at me, just as confused as I was. Who the hell would leave flowers on my step? There was a card with a note. I smiled, thinking that I had a secret admirer. I took out the card, smelled the flowers, and laid them on the desk.

"Read the card, girl!" Kiki yelled.

"Okay!" I replied.

I took the card out of the envelope and opened it. Once I did, I wished that I hadn't. Tears began to form in my eyes. Kiki and Black were both looking at me, wondering what the hell was wrong. I put my hand over my mouth and began to cry. How could this have happened?

"What's wrong, what does it say?" Black asked, moving close to me.

"It says, 'I hope you enjoyed the last two months—get ready for a war. You should have checked my pulse to see if I was dead.'" The note was handwritten and resembled Kemp's handwriting. I just knew this had to be a cruel joke.

"What?" Kiki looked at me, shocked.

Black snatched the note out of my hand and read it. He looked at me. I couldn't believe it. This had to be a cruel joke. There was no way that Kemp was alive. My body began to shake. I had to sit down before I fell to the ground. I sat in the chair sobbing. What was I going to do now? If Kemp was alive I was as good as dead. Then I thought about Black. He had gone in the house after me. Shit! That meant Kemp saw him. Now, not only would he be after me, but Black as well. I dragged him into this. I was numb, I couldn't think. Damn, why hadn't I checked his pulse? Why was I so sure that he'd died? Kiki looked as scared as me. Black was pacing the floor as if he was trying to come up with a plan. I hoped that he could. After a few minutes of pacing, he stopped in front of me.

"Don't worry, I'll take care of it."

I looked up at him and in my heart I believed him. I hoped that he could so that we could get on with our lives. I wanted things to go as planned. I wanted to continue being the head bitch in charge. I worked too hard for the title to lose it all.

Black Diamond 2: Nicety

Some call her Nice, but most call her Nasty

A Novel by **Brittani Williams**

Prologue

'*I hope you enjoyed the last two months get ready for a war. You should have checked my pulse to see if I was dead*' I couldn't believe my eyes nor could I believe such a thing was possible. Checked his pulse? Why hadn't I done that? I stood there in the office with both Kiki and Black staring me down waiting for me to tell them what the letter said. I had detached myself from the situation. I had instantly flashed back to that night and tried to figure out what I'd missed. Black went inside after me so he should have noticed. Did he see what I saw? I never really wanted to talk about it after that night but I just couldn't understand how I'd been so careless. Yes I was emotional but this could be the end for me, this could be the end for both Black and me.

"Don't worry, you'll take care of it?" I yelled.

'That's what I said, don't worry about it."

"How the hell do you expect me to do that? There's no way I can act like I didn't just read that fucking note. How the hell could this happen, Black? What the hell are we going to do?"

Kiki stood still as a statue, she couldn't believe it either. She warned me about this, she told me that I needed to be careful and now look what happened. I wanted her to say something. I wanted someone to say anything that made sense at this point because saying '*don't worry*' just wasn't going to get it. It just wasn't possible at a time like this.

"Didn't you see him Black? What did you see when you went inside the house?"

"Diamond, I just told you what happened."

"Well I need you to tell me again. Please tell me anything that would make this seem like a joke. This has to be a joke."

"I was sitting in the car when I saw you come out—I didn't see anyone else around. No cars or anything. I was sitting there waiting for Kemp to call me—we were supposed to go make a drop. I didn't know what the fuck was going on but I knew that something wasn't right. I waited until you pulled off and used the spare key Kemp gave me to go inside. I called his name and when I didn't get a response, I went upstairs and saw him laid out on the floor near the bed. I noticed that you tried to throw some things around but it looked staged so I hurried and ransacked the place a little more and then I left."

"He was on the floor?" I asked, from what I remembered he was on the bed so how the hell did he get on the floor?

"Yeah he was on the floor why does that matter?"

"Because, when I shot him he was on the bed.

How the hell could he have gotten on the floor unless he wasn't dead."

Black stood there with a puzzled look on his face. I was still trying to figure this out, there had to be something that we were missing. Kiki still stood in the same spot silent.

"He has to be dead, Diamond. It just doesn't make any sense."

"I know that it doesn't make sense but I know that someone knows something if they're sending shit like this."

"There was no one else there though. I sat outside and didn't see anyone else."

"The note clearly says something different." I was frustrated. This was something that I didn't need to deal with—I couldn't deal with it.

"D, I'm kind of thinking Black's right. I mean if he went in and saw him dead then it can't be him." Kiki finally chimed in though she wasn't saying anything that I wanted to hear.

This situation had me questioning everyone and everything. I wanted this to be over, I wanted to believe that everything was going to be okay but it didn't appear that way. I took the note from Black's hand and read it again—I still couldn't believe my eyes. I grabbed my bag off of the chair and headed towards the door without saying a word. I heard footsteps behind me but I didn't turn to look.

"Diamond, wait," Black yelled.

"What, Black? I need to get home right now so talk to me when you get there."

"Why are you angry at me? I'm not the one that's doing anything. Shit, you shot him. I just tried to help you cover it up."

I turned around and gave him the stare of death. "I didn't ask for your fucking help, I didn't ask you for anything."

"I didn't mean it like that, Diamond. I'm just trying to figure out why you're mad at me."

"I'm not mad at you, I'm mad at myself. I fucked up and now I could be killed. Look, I have to go. I'll talk to you at home."

"I'm going to follow you so just wait a minute. I don't feel comfortable with you traveling alone."

I didn't respond. I got in the car and drove off leaving him standing there. I didn't want to be followed. I didn't want to feel like a damn criminal or a child. I wanted shit to be normal. I looked in the rear view mirror and didn't see him. I needed some time alone. There wasn't anything that he could say to make me feel better. The only thing that would make me feel better was knowing Kemp's body was six feet under where I watched them lower it.

Chapter One: Diamond

Tricks of the Trade, November 2007

I had to see for myself. If I had the strength to dig six feet under I would have brought a shovel out here to this cemetery. It was cold and dark. Most people would think I was crazy for coming out here alone at 12 A.M. but for once in my life I could honestly admit that I was afraid. I had done too much to turn back or to even apologize for that matter. How could you say, "I'm sorry for shooting you?" The fact of the matter was that I wasn't sorry for shooting him, I was sorry that he hadn't died. I was confused—I could remember that day as if it were yesterday. I stood there at the foot of the bed as both Kemp and Mica's blood poured out onto the sheets and soaked into the bed. Someone was trying to scare me and it was definitely working.

He couldn't be alive, I didn't stay around to check his pulse but I knew it had to be him buried there. I put on an Oscar worthy performance at the funeral, even kissed his cold cheek. I was sure that I had gotten away with murder. What was I supposed to do now? I got down on my knees and put my hand on the head stone that read his name. So many things were running through my mind at this point. I wanted to pray but then I'd feel guilty for what I'd done to get me in this position in the first place. In my mind, things like this only happened in the movies, people who were assumed dead would return to cause a ruckus, but not in the real world. I was losing my mind—I had to know one way or another who the hell was screwing with me. Someone else must've been there that night—that was the only explanation that I could come up with. I heard leaves breaking as if someone were stepping on them and breaking them into pieces. I quickly turned my head and looked around and noticed no one. *What the hell was going on?* I thought.

"Who's there?" I spoke loudly enough to be heard but not too loud to wake up the neighborhood, I wasn't trying to bring more attention to myself. The cemetery on Lehigh Avenue was directly across from residential homes so I knew if I got too loud they could hear me. Then I thought, maybe that was a good thing, in case someone was trying to attack me. "Who's there?" I spoke again but still no answer. I focused my attention back on the headstone but at the same time I reached in my purse and held on to my gun to be safe.

"I know that I buried you. I just don't get it. Who's down there?" I heard the leaves again. I was getting annoyed. I stood up from the ground and looked around again. "Who the hell is out here?" Still no one answered.

Maybe I was just being paranoid. It was mid November and pretty windy out so it could have just been the wind blowing the leaves around. I looked at the headstone one last time before walking towards my car. I kept looking around the cemetery but with so many trees you could easily hide and not be seen. I still gripped on to my gun tightly as I walked so fast I was practically running. The sound of the leaves breaking got louder the faster I walked. My cell phone rang just as I pressed the keypad to unlock the car doors and damn near gave me a heart attack.

"Hello," I said as I hurried inside of the car and locked the doors.

"Babe, where the hell are you at?" Black yelled. I could tell that he was angry. With all of the stuff going on, he definitely didn't want me out of his sight. I ditched his security to come here. I couldn't stand to be followed.

"I'm on my way home. I'm just leaving the cemetery."

"The cemetery? What the hell would make you go to the cemetery at 12 A.M.? You need to get back here now."

"I just said I was on my way home." I knew he was worried but I wasn't a child. Hell, without me, he wouldn't have half of what he had now. He'd still be Kemp's understudy waiting for a chance to take the lead.

"Just hurry up!" He yelled into the receiver before hanging up. I didn't get a chance to respond but I was ready to curse him from A to Z. Shit, he should have learned from Kemp, no man was going to tell me what to do. Those days were long over. I started the car and tried to pull off but the car wouldn't move.

"What the hell?" I yelled. I got out and walked around to the back of the car and noticed both back tires were completely flat. Someone was definitely out here and the feeling of fear that came over my body damn near buckled my knees. I hurried back inside the car and dialed Black again.

"Come get me, somebody is out here trying to get me."

"What?"

"Black, just hurry up! Both of my back tires are flat and I heard someone following me. Please hurry up."

"I'm coming now."

I pulled my gun from my bag as I nervously sat and waited. I should have never been out there in the first place. Each time I saw movement I put my fingers in place to shoot. I laughed when it would end up being a tree branch or a plastic bag flying in the air. Was I tripping? Or was there really someone out there? I kept asking myself over and over again until something came crashing through my back window. Glass went everywhere and I heard footsteps going in the opposite direction. Once I could clearly see, I yelled, "I have a gun and trust me, I'll shoot!" I was scared shitless and I prayed that Black would pull up at any minute. My prayers were answered when I saw the headlights of his

BMW. I got out of the car and ran over almost knocking him over.

"Someone is trying to kill me, they threw something through my back window. I'm so glad you came." I hugged him and held on tight. The river of tears began to flow once I knew I was safe. He walked me over to the passenger seat of his car and put me inside. He walked over to my car and looked at the tires and windows before making a phone call. I wasn't sure who he called and honestly, I didn't care. I wanted him to get inside of the car and take me the hell home. I'd had enough excitement for one night. He was still on the phone when he climbed into the driver seat and drove off.

"All right get with me and let me know what's up. I need Merk to tow that car early. I don't need that shit getting any extra attention . . . Call me after he's done . . . I'm staying with her tonight and we'll link up tomorrow . . . alright one!" He turned and looked at me. I was still crying and shivering in my seat. He didn't say a word—he just reached over and put his hand on top of mine. I couldn't speak. I didn't know what to say. They say what goes around comes around and maybe it was my time to get what was coming for me. I walked into the house like a zombie. Black still didn't speak which was probably a good thing because I didn't know what to say. I sat down on the couch and soon he sat down next to me.

"I'm glad you're okay," he finally broke the silence but I didn't respond. I looked over at him and kissed him. Shit, I was more than glad that I was okay. I should have never been so foolish in the first place. I couldn't figure out what the hell possessed me to go out to a damn cemetery at night anyhow. Though he was a man and he wouldn't be one if he didn't do or say the stupid shit that men do, he was the one that I loved. I mean, none of the other men in my past truly cared about me the way that Black did. With training, Kemp probably could have but Black didn't need any of that, he did it on his own. It was then that I appreciated him even more. He could have went out to work which is what kept us living the lavish life but he chose to stay with me. We continued to kiss each other as if it were the last kiss we'd ever have. His hands were soon all over my body and my clothes had since hit the floor. His smooth skin next to mine felt like silk rubbing across my naked body. His movements were slow and deliberate and each touch hit spots that I didn't even realize could send chills up and down my spine. His body was sculpted to perfection. Every muscle looked like chocolate greatness as if it could melt in your mouth. I tried to relax and not exemplify how anxious I was but it was becoming more difficult to hold back with each second. His Sean John cologne was tickling my nose. I was in heaven waiting for him to reach my wet pussy and massage it as he'd done my nipples a few seconds earlier, but he chose to take his time. His hands slowly moved down my stomach and soon reached my throbbing clit, which was just about to erupt. My body began to shake on contact. The orgasm had been building up and just the slightest touch made me explode. Hell, he could have probably blown on it and gotten the same result.

I moved my hips to grind against his fingers as

he continued to kiss me sensually. At that point, I wished that I hadn't waited so long to get with him. I mean, when I met Kemp, Black was hanging in his shadow. I was looking for a leader so naturally Kemp caught my attention. Since money was my main objective, being with Black back then wasn't an option. All I could see were dollar signs. I married Kemp just for the money but being with Black was totally different, it was for love. Kemp had never been a slacker in the lovemaking department but it was just something about Black that I couldn't explain. I had never been with a man who could look at me and cause my lips to quiver. He was perfect in every sense of the word and when I felt his thick fingers slide inside of me I began to fuck them. I moaned loudly but was soon silenced as his lips touched mine and his tongue quickly followed behind. He stared me in the eye as if there was something that he wanted to say but couldn't find the words to speak. I wanted to know what was on his mind but I was enjoying the feeling of his fingers in my pussy too much to say a word.

"I love you," he whispered gently, almost like sweet poetry.

With just the sound of those two words my body began to shake and my juices were running down his fingers and forming a puddle in the palm of his hand. I wanted to return the favor but he didn't allow me to. He got on his knees and slowly pushed his dick inside of me. He wasn't fucking me like he had any other time. He was making love to me and I was making love to him. I could lie in that position forever, with him inside of me.

"I love you more," I finally whispered back after a few minutes of his slow lovemaking. With a slow lick of his ear and the tightening of my pussy walls he erupted inside of me. His sweat was dripping all over my face and I didn't even budge to wipe it off. I let it dry into my skin. I wanted all of him, even the perspiration from our lovemaking. After lying next to each other quietly for a few minutes the thoughts of my earlier encounter crossed my mind. I didn't want to fuck up the mood but I had to know what was on his mind and what his plan was. Shit, I could have been killed so I had every reason to be nervous.

"What are we going to do, Black? I mean, if he's really alive we're as good as dead." I was still lying next to him with my head nestled in his chest. I could hear his heart beating and surprisingly it hadn't skipped a beat.

"I told you I would take care of it. Kemp doesn't scare me, he never has but it can't be him, we both know that he's dead. I'm just focused on who the hell else knows what happened."

In a way I believed that what Black said was true but hell, everyone was afraid of Kemp—or at least I thought that they were. Black was strong and it was one of the things that I loved most about him. I mean who wanted to be with a wimp? Every woman wanted a man that could protect her. I wasn't crazy and I wanted to know who the culprit was just as much if not even more than Black.

"I know you told me that, Black, but we aren't together 24 hours a day. How can you protect me when you're not around? You see what just happened."

"I know we're not together all the time but I have eyes everywhere. You have to trust me. I won't let anything happen to you. I've got you now and I'm not letting you go. You just can't put yourself out there like that again, babe. You have to work with me until I figure out what the hell is going on here."

'Listen to him getting all sentimental', I thought. I smiled inside because for once I believed that it was true. I'd finally found a man that told me he loved me and meant it. Some would say that Kemp was in love with me and there were even some crazy people that would say Davey was too. I knew the truth and the fact of the matter is neither one of them really loved me. I was just something they could show off and be proud of. They could say that they made me and yes I admit it, they did make me. I didn't have shit before I met Davey and after my stint in prison I didn't have shit when I met Kemp either so it wasn't a lie that I still wouldn't have shit if it weren't for them.

See with Davey I was young and dumb. I fell for every word that he said and it didn't matter how many times he cheated or did me wrong, making up was always so good. He'd spoil me, he'd give me anything I wanted, and I couldn't turn any of that away. I was living the good life, shit, much better than that raggedy ass row home in North Philly. I had a huge apartment, a nice car, and a walk in closet full of designer clothes and shoes. Yeah, it sounds foolish but when you come from my background you cling on to things that feel better even though there are bumps along the way. I remember feeling like there was no other man for me and begged Davey to stay when he'd threaten to leave. Because of all of the drama in my life the nine months I spent in prison for Davey came to mind. That was the turning point in my life. Some would say that it wasn't in a good direction but I felt that it was. If you can emerge from a situation so devastating and come out on top it has to count for something. The days that I sat in my jail cell I had a lot of time to think. I thought about the time that he gave me the STD and defended the chick that he had locked in his bedroom nearly choking me to death. I thought about the time that he talked me into having a threesome, which later ended up sold on DVD in the streets. If that wasn't bad enough, I learned that the woman I had sex with, for him might I add, was the mother of his child—a child that I never knew he'd fathered. Then there was the straw that broke the camel's back. After doing a drop off for him I was arrested when it turned out to be a set up. So there I was in the detention center serving time and he didn't bother to answer my calls, letters, send me a penny, or pay me a visit. It was almost as if he'd forgotten about me the day that they took me in. I was distraught. What the hell was I supposed to do? When I came home, I was broke as a bum on the corner. I had no place, no money, clothes, or transportation. If it weren't for Kiki, I would have either landed in a shelter or back in North Philly with my hating ass aunt Cicely and all of her damn kids! I had to do something—something to survive. So any critic that thought I was wrong for searching out a man like Kemp in order to get to the top, they could pucker up and kiss my ass because they weren't in my shoes to say what I should or shouldn't have done. Buy hey, if I wouldn't have met Kemp, I wouldn't have met Black and that's the wonderful thing— the thing that kept me smiling.

Black got off the sofa and I knew that it was time for work. Damn, I wanted to enjoy this moment. Being the head of an empire had its downfalls too. You never really get too much quality time. He walked upstairs to the bathroom as I lay there watering at the mouth. His body was a masterpiece. The muscles in his back were sculpted to perfection. His skin was smooth as melted chocolate and the sweat from our lovemaking gave his body just the right amount of shine. His ass was perfect too. I'd never seen an ass on a man like his. I just wanted to lie next to it all day long. Within a few seconds I heard the shower running and following that I smelled his Sean John body wash filling the air. I inhaled and got chills. I wanted to go meet him in the shower for round two but I knew he had to go to work. I rolled over and closed my eyes, I wasn't sleepy but my mind was exhausted. I knew that I would drive myself crazy trying to figure out how the hell I had gotten myself into this mess. I was so careful, well at least I thought that I was. Black emerged from the bathroom about 15 minutes later with a towel wrapped around his waist. By then I was sitting on the edge of the bed in the bedroom.

"Are you gonna be okay? If not I'll get JB to send

someone over here. Matter fact, I will have him do that anyway. I don't want to leave you here alone."

Though I wasn't really comfortable having the workers in my house, it was the best thing to do. I knew that I wouldn't have been able to rest anyway wondering if someone would creep in here while I was asleep and kill me. It may sound silly, but it was the truth—I was scared shitless.

"That's fine, I'd feel better with someone here anyway," I agreed. Black walked toward the closet and began to get dressed. I just sat there admiring him. I wondered how I'd gotten so lucky and found a man like him. I wished that I had found him a long time ago. Maybe then I wouldn't be sitting here fearing for my life. After he'd finished getting dressed he walked over to my side of the bed and kissed me good-bye.

I fell asleep and woke up around 7 A.M. to a ringing cell phone. *Who the hell was calling me so early?* I fumbled through my bag, which was lying on the bedside table to find it.

"Hello," I said, in a low tone. I hadn't even fully opened my eyes yet. There were specks of light peeping in through the blinds which nearly gave me a headache—probably from my lack of sleep.

"Babe, you won't believe this shit!" Black's loud voice woke me up instantly.

"What? What happened?" I was nervous. I didn't really want to hear the answer as I sat up in bed and fought with the sun to fully open my eyes.

"The fucking store on Hunting Park is burning down! I need to know what muthafucker had something to do with this. When I find his ass it's going to be a war for real."

"The store is burning down?" I couldn't believe it. I mean it wasn't as if it was a big money spot but shit it did make money. What the hell were they trying to prove? This is definitely not what I wanted to wake up to. I knew things could only get worse from that point on. I was second guessing myself again. Who else but Kemp would have something to gain by terrorizing us? That night flashed in front of me like a film on television. I walked into my house as I did on any other day but when I pulled up in the driveway I noticed the car we'd let Mica use while she was working on getting back on her feet. It was strange because we hadn't seen each other in five years but in a few short weeks we'd become closer than we were before. In a way, I still felt bad about the fact that her brother murdered their father but I knew as well as she, that I had no part of that. I loved her brother, and there was no way I'd want him to land in prison for the rest of his life. Maybe I shouldn't have trusted that our relationship could get back on track. Maybe I was a fool for thinking a woman couldn't possibly be interested in the person that murdered her man right in front of her. There I was walking up the stairs with my heart beating a hundred beats a minute. I felt in my heart that something was wrong. Okay, yes I planned to get rid of Kemp but I never thought I'd get betrayed by her.

As I made my way down the hall I could see the flickering of a candle and could hear the faint sounds of moaning. I walked slowly to avoid being heard. I almost burst when I saw her straddled on top of him. I instantly wanted to speak, yell, scream, or do something other than what I was doing. I was

standing there like a statue. My body was doing
something totally different than my mind. In my
mind I was moving in on them letting my presence
be known but my feet weren't budging. Instead, I
stuck my hand into my bag and pulled out my
handgun—a handgun which I carried for protec-
tion. This protective tool was now a weapon and
before I knew it, blood was spraying all over the bed,
walls, and pretty much every surface in the room.
I didn't know what to do next. My first thought
was to throw things around and make the house
appear to have been robbed. I didn't bother to check
and make sure they were both dead. All I could
think about was getting out of the house without
being seen. I hurried out of the house and returned just in enough time to find the police and
ambulances scattered all around the driveway and
lawn. I put on the performance of the grieving wife
and was picked up by Kiki who took me over to her
apartment for the night. By the note and the recent incidents, I was sure someone knew what I'd
done—but who? But then, I was so disoriented I
didn't even notice Black in his car watching me
run into the car in a sweat suit carting a hand full
of trash bags. I could have missed someone else.
Hell, he could have missed someone else.

I was becoming angrier by the minute and the
conversation with Black wasn't going that great either. I wanted to know what the hell was going on
as I snapped back to reality.

"Yeah, I'll talk to you about it when I get home.
I'm trying to wrap shit up with the cops now."

"Black—"

"I'll talk to you when I get home, I have to go."

Click.

I sat there and stared at the phone. I was tempted to call him back. I wanted to know what the hell was going on with my store. It just didn't make sense to me and Black's attitude wasn't making things any better. Yes, he ran the businesses but shit, I owned everything so technically he worked for me. So the fact that he was being so brief was really pissing me off. I got up out of bed and rummaged through my closet for something to wear. I had to go down to the store and see it for myself. Black would be pissed but hell, I was pissed right now so he'd just have to deal with me being there. I put on a Juicy Couture sweat suit and headed out of the door. I still had to look the part since there'd probably be cameras and shit at the scene. I couldn't be caught slipping not even on a bad day. I sped down to the store in the Mercedes Benz Black bought me last month, which was a good thing since my Jaguar was sitting on two flats. I immediately noticed the yellow tape and police officers blocking off the scene. I could only get within a two-block radius. I parked and got out to walk over. Black smoke filled the air and you could see the three fire trucks pouring water on to the building. People were crowding around trying to get a glimpse of the building. I heard a few old ladies talking as I walked by.

"There she goes right there. I'm glad that fucking store is burning."

"Yes, keep the drugs off of our block!"

I didn't respond. I didn't even turn around to see who said what. It didn't matter. I knew how they felt—I felt that way once. I lived in a neighborhood full of drug dealers and crack heads and I hated it. So I'm sure people would wonder how I could grow up and fall into the same line of work. Well the answer is pretty simple, money. Money was my motivation and after all that I'd been through there wasn't any other job out there for me. I saw Black, JB, and a few other workers in a huddle near the corner. I walked over.

"What are you doing here?" He yelled.

"I had to see the store for myself."

"You don't need to be here." He grabbed me by the arm so we could walk away from the workers.

"Yes I do, Black, It's my store."

"Okay, now you've seen it you can go home."

"I'm not going anywhere."

"Why do you have to be so stubborn? Just go home and I'll take care of it."

I stood there silent. I wanted to believe that he could but I wasn't so sure looking at the building burning to the ground. Whoever it was definitely wasn't going to stop until we were both out of the picture. I wasn't going to stand out there in front of everyone and argue with him so I agreed to leave and quietly headed toward my car. I was angry. Not at Kemp or Black but at myself for letting this happen. I got in the car and looked around to see if I saw anyone suspicious. Who the hell was I looking for? For some reason, I still hoped I'd see Kemp. At least that way we'd know who to look for. I didn't really think they'd be stupid enough to hang around the scene but shit, that could be cockiness too. If it were Kemp, he knew we'd never turn him into the cops after what I'd done to him and Mica and if it wasn't him we wouldn't know where to start pointing the finger anyway. I was paranoid. I started the car to drive home. I had to clear my head. I couldn't live the rest of my life looking over my shoulders wondering when someone was going to kill me. I had to focus on something else so that I could move on with my life. Black wouldn't let anything happen to me. He promised me that and I had to believe him. I had to obtain that thug mentality that men have, the one that sheds all of the fear. I had to learn the *tricks of the trade* if I wanted to make it in this business.